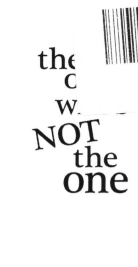

the
c
w
NOT
the
one

BOOKS BY KERIS STAINTON

the one who's NOT the one

KERIS STAINTON

bookouture

Published by Bookouture in 2019

An imprint of StoryFire Ltd.

Carmelite House
50 Victoria Embankment
London EC4Y 0DZ

www.bookouture.com

ISBN: 978-1-78681-458-6
eBook ISBN: 978-1-78681-457-9

*For Emily and Martina *finger guns**

PROLOGUE

Then...

Cat had been lying awake for at least an hour before she decided to get up. The house was too quiet. There was no way she was going to get back to sleep. She couldn't even get her eyes to close.

Sam was lying on his back, one arm behind his head, the other across his chest, his forehead furrowed in a frown. She thought about waking him, but instead she swung her legs out of bed, pulled on Sam's hoodie, and tiptoed out of the room.

If she was at home, she'd have to use the light on her phone to avoid the bags and boxes and other random detritus scattered around, but Sam's mum's place was like Kelly's – everything was perfect and tidy and organised. In the daytime, Cat found it comforting, but at night something about it bugged her. She went to the bathroom, peed, and stared at herself in the mirror, swiped at the dark circles under her eyes with her thumbs, pushed her hands back through her hair, sighed.

She needed a cup of tea.

There was enough moonlight coming through the windows on the landing and at the bottom of the stairs that she didn't need to put a light on, so she padded down in her bare feet and headed for the kitchen, flicking the light on as she pushed the door open.

'Shit!' Harvey yelled from the dining table, pushing his chair back and making the legs screech across the tile.

'Fuck ME,' Cat yelped, her heart racing. 'Oh my GOD.'

Harvey was already laughing, a hand over his eyes. 'Turn it off.'

Cat flicked the light back off again and closed the door behind her as she stepped into the room.

'What the fuck?'

Harvey was sitting at the dining table, his curly hair pointing in every direction, his hand no longer covering his face, which, Cat could see, was puffy from sleep.

'I couldn't sleep,' Harvey said. 'Although I was just starting to drift off when you scared the living shit out of me.'

Cat laughed. 'I scared you? I wasn't expecting anyone else to be up. I nearly wet myself.'

'Sorry. Do you think anyone heard?'

Cat scoffed. 'We both screamed like little girls, so I'd be surprised if they didn't.' She stared at him for a second. 'I was just going to make a tea. Do you want one?'

'I was, um…' He scratched the back of his neck. 'Actually, yeah. Tea sounds good. I'll do it.'

He pushed his chair back again and made to stand up.

'You're OK,' Cat said. 'I can.'

She wanted something to focus on that wasn't Harvey, in the kitchen, in a T-shirt and shorts, looking soft and sleepy and really really hot.

'You couldn't sleep either?' Harvey asked, as Cat filled the kettle. 'I mean… obviously you couldn't.'

'I woke up,' Cat said without turning round. 'And then that was it. Wide awake.'

'Sam snoring?'

Cat laughed. 'Nah. Fast asleep though. He can sleep through anything.'

She turned to glance at the door then. 'Seems like we didn't wake anyone up after all.'

'Just Dusty,' Harvey said, and Cat saw the family cat had hopped up onto Harvey's lap.

'Hey,' Harvey said in a sing-song voice. 'Human Cat is making tea.'

'Don't you start,' Cat said. Sam had started the 'Human Cat' thing and thought he was very funny. 'Mind if I turn the oven light on?'

'S'fine,' Harvey said. 'It was just the big light. It's really fucking bright.'

The light from the cooker hood bathed the countertop in a warm orange while Cat finished making the tea and then took it over to the table where Harvey was nuzzling Dusty, who'd already had enough and was trying to get away from him.

'What about you?' Cat asked Harvey. 'Reason you're not asleep right now?'

'Oh, I just, you know, woke up and started thinking about how I don't know what I want to do with my life. Nothing important.' He smiled, dipping his head, his hair falling down over his face.

Dusty jumped down and ran to the door. Harvey got up to let her out and Cat found herself staring at his legs. They were nice. She looked down into her tea.

'I thought you wanted to be a…' Cat frowned. 'Sound engineer?'

'Lighting,' Harvey said.

'Ironic. Since you shrivelled like a Gremlin when I turned that light on.'

Harvey smiled. 'At work no one usually beams a light into my face when I'm almost asleep.'

'Sorry,' Cat said.

'And my girlfriend dumped me,' Harvey added, dipping his head and rubbing the back of his neck again.

'Ah,' Cat said. 'God. Sorry. Why did she…?' Cat couldn't imagine what kind of girl wouldn't want to go out with Harvey. He was sweet and funny and cute and, if he was anything like his brother, good in bed. That was a weird thought. She drank some tea and tried to un-think it.

'Yeah. She was… I mean, she's right. We weren't… It's just…'

'Have you ever thought about public speaking,' Cat teased.

Harvey sat up straight and stretched his arms over his head, smiling at her across the table. 'I'm tired, OK? I'm not at my best.'

'You should go back to bed.'

Harvey lifted his tea and looked at her over the top of the mug. 'Got to finish my tea, haven't I.'

An alarm buzzed on his phone and he glanced down at it before pushing his chair back again and standing up.

'Want to see something cool?'

'Oh, my mum warned me about people like you,' Cat said, and immediately regretted it.

Harvey grinned at her. 'We have to go outside.'

'Kinky.'

Harvey was already opening the back door, so Cat followed him out into the garden.

'Perfect night for it,' Harvey said, looking up.

'For a murder?' Cat asked, rolling the r.

'International Space Station,' Harvey said, heading further out into the middle of the lawn.

'You set an alarm in the middle of the night to look at the International Space Station?' Cat asked, following him and looking up too. The sky was dotted with bright stars. 'How will you know it?'

'You'll see,' Harvey said. 'It's unmistakeable. And, no, I don't set an alarm. It's an alert. It wouldn't have woken me up if I hadn't had my phone… there, look.'

Cat looked where he was pointing and saw what looked like a bright white star moving smoothly and surprisingly quickly above them in an arc.

'Holy shit.'

She knew without looking at him that Harvey had turned to grin at her. 'I know, right?'

'That is not what I was expecting. Like... what is it?'

'It's the International Space Station.'

Cat glanced at him. His head was tipped back and she took the opportunity to look at the long line of his throat, his Adam's apple bobbing slightly as he swallowed.

'Yeah, but is it a satellite? There's not, like, people on it?'

Harvey looked at her, nodding. 'There is, yeah. I don't know who right now, but you remember Commander Hadfield? He was on it.'

'Yeah. God. I thought he was on a...' She wanted to say rocket. There was no way she was going to say rocket. 'Something else. Something stationary.'

'Nope,' Harvey said. 'It's constantly circling the earth. It's really fucking cool.'

Cat glanced at the white dot again and then back at Harvey. Even in the dark, she could see his eyes sparkling.

'You really love it,' she said.

He looked at her, smiling. 'I do, yeah. I just can't imagine what that would be like. Being up there, looking down at all of us, down here. Seeing the earth – all of it – every single day. They see like sixteen sunsets and sunrises every day, something like that.'

Cat had no idea how that could possibly work, but instead she said, 'Wow.'

'Yeah,' Harvey replied. 'Wow is the word.'

CHAPTER ONE

Now...

'I'm still thinking about the exploding bee genitals,' Cat said into her phone.

The man sitting opposite her on the Tube who'd been rustling the *Metro* and tutting at every page, looked up at her and frowned. She resisted the urge to pull a face at him.

'Why?' Kelly said.

Cat could tell her friend was distracted. She shouldn't phone her in the mornings – Kelly had to get herself and Arnold up and dressed and out of the house for school – but Cat just got so bloody bored on her commute.

'Because they make a sound! It's mad enough that they blow their own balls off when they shag, but that the explosion is audible to the human ear? The fuck is that?'

'What a world,' Kelly said.

'Am I on speaker?' Cat asked, hearing the echo of Kelly's enormous kitchen.

'Of course you're on speaker. I'm doing Arnold's lunch.'

Cat knew that Kelly wouldn't be making the kind of packed lunches she used to get – a jam sandwich and a few chocolate fingers if she was lucky. No, Kelly was probably making something ridiculously creative.

'What's he having?' Cat asked.

'Mediterranean salad jar,' Kelly told her. 'I'm chopping a red pepper.'

'Will he eat that?' The woman sitting next to Cat crossed her legs, kicking Metro Man in the shin. He rustled his paper again.

'Course,' Kelly said. 'He loves it.'

'Weird kid,' Cat said, but she smiled into her phone. Arnold was her godson and the love of her life. Probably. 'Tell him I'll bring him a family bag of Skittles next time I come round.'

'You will not.'

'Gotta go,' Cat said. 'Going underground.'

'Have a good day,' Kelly said.

Cat spent the rest of her commute playing Two Dots on her phone (occasionally forgetting where she was and muttering 'For fuck's sake!' aloud). She always planned to use the time to read or draft emails to friends she hadn't been in touch with for too long, but the lure of distraction was too strong.

After getting off the train, Cat stood on the Tube platform and considered whether she had the time or inclination to go and get coffee. And maybe a pastry. She should go straight to work – she was meant to start at ten and it was five to – but most of the male managers just wandered in whenever they felt like it and no one ever questioned it. Cat, however, was used to being conscientious. It had always been her downfall.

Her stomach rumbled, making her mind up for her. She'd planned to have breakfast at home, but she'd opened the fridge to find the milk gone. But the empty plastic jug had been put back in the fridge. Her flatmate, Georgie. Or, more likely, Georgie's dickhead boyfriend. She really should move out. Or ask Georgie to move out. Or for her dickhead boyfriend to not stay over so much at the very least. But she never did. Because she was a massive wuss.

Five minutes later, Cat came out of Starbucks trying to balance her own latte, an Americano for her boss, Colin (because if she was going to be late – and she was – she might as well suck up a bit too), a cheese and tomato toastie, napkins, sugar sachets and a stirrer.

'Got your hands full there,' a man sitting at the nearest outside table said.

'Right? I didn't think this through. Is it OK if I just…' She was already putting everything down by the time she actually looked at him and, woah, he was really hot. Brown eyes and dark hair that was flopping over his forehead. A hint of stubble and a cheeky grin.

'Help yourself.' He gestured at the table.

He was smoking, which Cat wasn't a huge fan of, but she could work with it. She put her purse on the table as she opened her bag to put the toastie in and took the top off her coffee to add sugar.

'Do you work round here?' the guy asked. He narrowed his eyes as he took a drag of his cigarette and Cat was appalled to find it made him look even hotter.

Cat smiled. 'Yeah, not far. You?'

He shrugged a little, smirking again and Cat wondered if Colin would accept 'I met a cute guy and did a bit of flirting' as a reason for lateness. Maybe if she added 'And I bought you an Americano! Ta-da!'

'Maybe I'll see you around?' he said, pushing his chair back and standing.

'Maybe.' Cat smiled up at him.

Maybe they could meet here each morning before work, Cat fantasised, as she watched him walk away – nice tight bum hugged by black jeans. Buy their coffees separately and chat a little until one day she'd arrive and he'd have already bought her latte and she'd offer to return the favour, but he'd say, 'How about a real drink?' And then they'd… shit. Where was her purse? On the table was her latte, Colin's Americano, the empty sugar packet and stirrer. No purse. She must have put it in her bag. But she couldn't see it. She took out the toastie, a pair of spare knickers she'd had in there for, god, possibly years, three haphazardly folded issues of *Stylist* magazine, a pen, two frayed phone chargers, one of those bags that folded up into a strawberry that had been part of her (shit) Secret Santa at work last year, a perfume sample, a packet of tampons, and an empty water bottle. But no purse.

'Shit,' she said. And then, louder, 'SHIT.'

'Y'alright, love?' the man on the fruit and veg stall called.

'That guy I was talking to?' Cat said. 'I think he stole my purse.'

She still couldn't quite believe it though. Maybe it had fallen under the table or she'd put it in her pocket or… No. It was gone. He must have taken it.

'Come here and I'll give you a banana. For free,' the fruit man said and waggled his eyebrows.

'Now's not the time!' Cat said, muttering 'for fuck's sake' under her breath.

At least she still had her phone. She called Kelly.

'You will not believe what just happened,' she said, as soon as her friend picked up.

'Doing a half day?' Cat's boss, Colin, said without looking up from his desk. The office smelled like soup, even though it was only half ten.

Cat gave a feeble laugh at his feeble joke, before saying, 'I've just been mugged!'

Colin's head shot up from where he'd been staring down at his laptop. 'What? Seriously? Shit!'

Cat nodded. She actually felt much better than she had just after it had happened. She'd drunk her latte and eaten her toastie and talked to Kelly. She'd almost stopped shaking.

'I got you a coffee,' Cat said. 'But I dropped it when… it happened.'

That wasn't actually true. She'd thrown it away because by the time she'd finished hers it had gone cold, but it was the thought that counted.

'Are you hurt?' Colin asked, emerging from his office. It was such an unusual occurrence that heads popped up throughout the room. 'Do you need to go to hospital? Or the police! Did you call the police?'

Cat shook her head. 'I'm fine. I'm not hurt. It was just… a shock, you know?' She sat down at her own desk. 'I didn't think about the police. Should I call them? I don't know what they can do. He'll be long gone now.'

'Have you cancelled your cards?' Colin asked.

Cat shook her head. 'Not yet.' There was so little money in her bank account that it hadn't seemed urgent.

'Right, you should do that,' Colin said. 'Mate of mine got his wallet nicked once and by the time he'd realised it had gone, they'd helped themselves to over six grand.'

Cat stared at him, the idea of having anything close to six grand in her bank account completely alien.

'Wow,' she said. 'That's shit.'

Colin nodded. 'So, yeah, cancel your cards and then I need the Blacklers file, if you've got it to hand.'

'No problem,' Cat said. 'Actually it's here.'

She slid open the desk drawer to her right and handed him the file. He blinked down at it for a second before saying, 'Right. Great. Thanks,' and heading back towards his office. He stopped in the doorway and turned back to look at Cat.

'Nick's coming in this afternoon,' he said. 'Are you free?'

Cat flicked open the red hardback notebook she used as a diary and ran her finger down the blank page.

'Should be,' she said.

Colin gave her a thumbs up and closed his office door behind him.

Cat kicked off her shoes and pulled her feet up so she was sitting cross-legged in her chair. She stared at her reflection in the black screen of her computer. She felt... weird. Shaken. Even though pretty much everyone she knew had been mugged at some point and it could have been so much worse. She tried to take a mental inventory of her purse, but beyond her debit card, a credit card that was forever up to its limit, and various shop loyalty cards, she couldn't think of what else she might have lost.

She wondered idly why Nick was coming in. He worked in RMJ's other branch in Soho Square. Cat had originally interviewed at that branch and she'd been excited to work in those offices, right in the centre of town. This branch – off Tottenham Court Road and overlooking Bedford Square – was cool too, if a little Dickensian, particularly in winter. Nick was one of the few people at RMJ that Cat actually liked, even though he often made her madly nervous. He was just so hot. And funny. And, apparently, good at his job. For his birthday, Cat had given him a card featuring a glittery unicorn and hoped he got what it meant. For her birthday, he'd given her a card that said 'Happy Birthday to the World's Best Wife' and he'd added 'Work' above 'Wife'.

She googled the phone number for her bank and, while she was on hold for the card cancellation line, doodled in her notebook. By the time the card was cancelled and a new one ordered, she'd covered an entire page with variations of the word 'Nick'. Some in bubble writing, some scored over so many times it had come through to the next page, and some, embarrassingly, surrounded by tiny misshapen hearts. She ripped the page out and fed it into the shredder under her desk.

She needed another coffee.

'So this is exciting news,' Nick said, sitting at the end of the conference room table.

Cat was sitting to his left and Colin to his right with the other three account managers making up the rest of the table.

'I think some of you probably had an idea that this was on the cards,' Nick added.

Cat's stomach clenched, thinking he might be about to attempt to spin closure and redundancies as 'exciting'.

'As you know part of the reason for the merger with Jonas was to expand internationally and we're starting with...' The fact that he paused for drama was one of the things Cat loved about Nick. 'New York.'

'Oh, shiiiiiit,' Cat said before she could stop herself.

'I know, right?' Nick grinned at her. 'There will be opportunities for secondment – case-based – but I'm actually going to be based out there permanently.'

'No!' Cat said, again before she could stop herself. What was wrong with her? She bit at her lips and stared ahead through the windows at Bedford Square.

'I'm sorry.' Nick smiled. 'Try not to hate me too much.'

Cat looked back at him to find him still grinning. He thought she was jealous he was moving to New York. Right. Good. She didn't want him to know he was the only person who made her job tolerable. (Although she suspected she may have hinted about it at the previous year's Christmas party.) But she should have known anyway.

'Tell you what though,' Nick said, 'I'm going to have a fantastic leaving do.'

Of course, Cat thought.

And she should have seen it coming.

All men leave eventually. Some of them even take your purse with them.

CHAPTER TWO

After the office meeting, Nick hung around a little, eventually sitting in the chair on the other side of Cat's desk, and chatted a little about the New York move. He'd lived there during a year out before university and had wanted to get back for a while.

'I've never been,' Cat said.

'Oh you should.' Nick smiled and picked up a paperclip from Cat's desk, immediately straightening it then starting to bend it again. 'You'd love it. It's the most exciting place.'

Cat used to think London was the most exciting place. That's why she'd moved there. But the novelty had worn off over the last few years. She wondered if anyone ever got sick of New York.

'It'll be weird though,' Nick said. 'Not being able to come and bother you.'

Cat nodded. It really would. Before the merger, when Rogers & Mitchell were in their old office, they'd had their own receptionist, Yvonne, rather than a main reception for the whole building. One day she'd emailed Cat asking her to come out to reception; she wanted to 'test something'. Cat had rolled her eyes, sighed heavily, heaved herself out of her chair and taken the ten steps through the double doors to reception, where she found Yvonne wide-eyed at someone sitting on the sofa.

'What's up?' Cat asked.

Yvonne nodded at the person on the sofa and waggled her eyebrows at Cat. Cat assumed it was either a celebrity (which was unlikely, but not impossible; they'd done some tax work for someone off *Made in Chelsea*, and Colin had given VAT advice to someone who said they were working for Danny Baker), or an ex of Yvonne's. Cat turned just in time to see the guy stretch out his legs and lean back on the sofa, his hips lifting slightly, elongating his thighs, the small of his back arching up as his shoulders pressed down, the long line of his throat—

'What the fuck?' Cat muttered under her breath.

'I know!' Yvonne said and then made shoo hands at Cat.

Cat shooed back to her desk, sat down, wiggled a bit, and emailed *WHAT THE FUCK* to Yvonne.

I thought it was just me. He's the sexiest man I've ever seen in real life. Right? RIGHT?

Cat nodded pointlessly at her computer, before replying with shaking hands. *Would it be unprofessional to come out there and straddle him?*

You'd have to fight me first.

And then the doors had opened and he'd walked into the office, nodded at Cat, who may or may not have emitted a small squeak, and strolled into Colin's office.

Five minutes later, Cat had another email from Yvonne and it contained a link to his Facebook page. Nick's Facebook page. Nick Ivory. His profile photo was black and white and he appeared to be wearing a Hawaiian shirt, but it was probably designer (she'd subsequently found out it was Prada – almost seven hundred quid for a shirt he could probably have got in Topman for less than twenty). In one hand he was holding an empty wine glass, the other was curled around a cigarette. He was staring at the camera like he was challenging it. Cat didn't know how the person who'd taken the photo could possibly still be alive. Surely they must have died of the horn instantly?

Cat had wanted to download it and set it as her phone wallpaper, but she knew that even for her that was a bit much. But god.

That had been two years ago. Since then, she'd spent lots of time with him in the office and a little time out of the office on various work dos and while he was still the sexiest man she'd ever met, she could at least now talk to him without panting. She liked him. And he was moving to New York. Work would be much less fun. And her wank bank would be horribly depleted.

Metro Man was on the same Tube on the way home. When Cat had first started commuting, she'd liked seeing the same people every day, had even harboured some fantasies about befriending the woman with the blonde bob, star-sprinkled jumpsuit and red ankle boots, or maybe the guy with the closely trimmed beard who was reading a different novel every single morning would ask her for a coffee. She'd most likely say no, but it would be nice to be asked. But she'd soon learned that a tight smile or quick nod was the most she was going to get from anyone. Most of the time, everyone avoided eye contact as much as possible.

Cat stood and waited for the train to pull into Queen's Park station. There was always a bit of a scrum to get off and people never seemed to learn that if they just waited it would be fine. Someone bumped the back of her knee with a bag and she glanced over her shoulder, intending to give them a hard stare, but instead something caught her eye in Metro Man's paper.

'Excuse me,' she said, leaning over and tapping the top of the paper. 'Could you just turn back to the previous page?'

'No?' the man said, flicking the paper closed and shoving it in his bag.

'Very helpful,' Cat said. 'Thank you so much.'

She was still muttering to herself about Tube wankers when she reached the platform and spotted a *Standard* abandoned on a bench. She sat down and opened it, flicking through the pages until... yes. She was right. It was him. Sam. Her ex, Sam. In the paper.

She called Kelly.

'I really can't talk right now, babe,' Kelly said. 'I'm just popping out to—'

'Sam's in the *Standard*,' Cat interrupted.

'Your Sam? OK, just give me a minute.'

Cat heard Arnold talking in the background. His pipey little voice made her heart hurt.

'Give Arnold a kiss for me, eh?' she told Kelly.

'Roger that,' Kelly said.

Cat laughed when she heard Arnold say, 'Get off me!' And then the car doors opening and closing.

'Right, I'm in the car,' Kelly said. 'Tell me quick. Has he killed someone?'

'I wish,' Cat said, even though she didn't. Obviously. 'He's back in London, I guess. And doing a stand-up gig.'

'What?'

'I know, right?'

'Sam? Your Sam?'

'Hang on,' Cat said. She read the article again while in her ear she heard the car start, Arnold say, 'I dropped my banana!' and Kelly's, 'Hang on a second, sweetpea.'

The headline was *Sam Salt Puts the Cat Among the Pigeons*. It was basically just a puff piece promoting his show; there wasn't much information to be had. But there was a photo.

'He looks good,' Cat said, her voice breaking halfway through.

'Don't google him!' Kelly almost-yelled. 'I mean it, Cat. I'll ring back in a bit, OK?'

'OK,' Cat said.

'Bye, Cat!' Arnold shouted.

'Bye, babe.'

After ending the call, she had to force herself to put her phone back in her bag. Her fingers were almost twitching to tap on Safari, to type in 'Sam Salt' and then 'image search'. Instead she stared at the photo in the paper. It was a professional shot, not a photo she'd ever seen before. Sam was in focus in the middle, the background – a red stage curtain – slightly blurred. He was looking directly into the camera and smirking. It was what Cat used to call his Kermit smile, his mouth curled up on one side. And his eyes – she moved the paper from side to side – yep, his eyes followed you. Great. His hair was tufty, sticking up at the front. She remembered smoothing it down in the morning when… No. She wasn't going to think about that.

She closed the paper and placed it on the bench next to her. Then she picked it up again and flicked back to Sam's photo. Brown leather jacket. She hadn't seen that before. He didn't have it when they were together. She wondered where he'd bought it. If it was vintage. His eyebrows looked good. She sort of wanted to brush her thumb over them. She used to do that. She used to brush both thumbs over them at once while saying, '*Augenbrow*!' – German for eyebrows. Probably. She'd never looked it up. She'd seen it or read it or heard it and thought it was funny. She couldn't even remember where. Whenever she did it, Sam would press her nose like a bell and say '*Igelschnäuzchen*', which meant 'little hedgehog snout'. And he would never tell her how he knew that. She hadn't thought about that for so long. Had stopped thinking of stuff like that when he'd fucked off to Australia.

When Kelly phoned back, Cat was still sitting on the bench. She was cold and her bum was damp, but she just hadn't been able to make herself get up. She'd made a plan – she was going to go straight to Londis and buy a bottle of wine – but she hadn't managed to stand yet.

'Do you need me to come and get you?' Kelly asked.

'No,' Cat said. 'Thanks. I'm fine. I'll be fine. As soon as I can get off this bench.'

'Listen,' Kelly said. 'You and Sam… it's a long time ago.'

'Five years,' Cat said.

'Right. And you're doing good, right?'

'Am I fuck.'

'Right,' Kelly said. 'But you're OK. You've got a home and a job and friends that you love. And Arnold.'

'I live in a tiny room in a shared flat with people I cross the road to avoid. The only good thing in my job is fucking off to New York – oh, I haven't even told you about that! I haven't had a boyfriend since Sam, haven't had sex for two years and I can't even remember the last time someone kissed me.'

'Presumably it was when you had sex?' Kelly suggested.

'You'd think so, wouldn't you? But no.'

A woman in a bright yellow raincoat waiting for the next train shuffled further along the platform away from Cat.

'Everything's been shit since Sam,' Cat said.

'Oh god,' Kelly said. 'Is that the story you're telling yourself? Stay where you are. I'm going to come and get you. We can get a takeaway and a bottle of wine. Stay over.'

'I'm going to get wine. Once I stand up.'

'OK, good,' Kelly said. 'You do that then. I'll come and pick you up outside Londis.'

'You won't be able to stop outside Londis. You'll have to pull into the car park. You know, on the corner.'

'Yeah. I know. Don't worry. OK? Just stand up.'

'I will.'

'No, I mean now. Stand up now. And don't just say you have. Do it.'

Cat stood up, leaving the paper on the bench next to her. 'I'm standing up.'

'Can you get yourself to the Londis?'

Cat glanced back at the bench and thought about sitting back down again. Instead, she made herself put one foot in front of the other until she was walking up the steps.

'You can let me go now,' Cat said. 'I'll go to Londis. We've said Londis too many times now. Sounds weird.'

'OK, good. I'll see you soon. Well, I'll be about half an hour. Love you.'

'Love you too.'

While Cat waited for Kelly she tried not to think about how Sam had left. How he'd gone to Australia for a year and ended up staying for five. How her dad had gone to Australia twenty years earlier and had never come back. How depressing it was that both of them had felt the need to go to the other side of the world to get away from her.

She tried not to think about any of that.

She failed miserably.

CHAPTER THREE

'Cat!' Arnold yelled, running down the hall and smacking right into Cat's midriff.

'Bloody hell, kid,' she said, winded. 'Are you trying to kill me?'

She picked him up, even though he was too big to be picked up really, and he wrapped his legs around her waist like a chimpanzee.

'I told you to be careful!' Kelly said, passing the two of them and heading straight for the kitchen.

'I'm doing my best!' Cat called back. Arnold laughed against her neck and she sniffed his hair. He always smelled really good, which was ridiculous since he was actually a grotty, sweaty kid who quite often had glue in his hair and ketchup on his face.

'You smell like...' Cat gave another huge sniff.

'School?' Arnold guessed.

'Antarctica,' Cat suggested. 'I'm getting snow and ice and...' She sniffed again. 'Penguin poo.'

In Kelly's enormous, ridiculously gorgeous kitchen, Cat sat him down on the breakfast island and said, 'You can stay there, right?'

Arnold nodded enthusiastically as Kelly said, 'Get him down.'

'Killjoy,' Cat said. She lifted Arnold down and watched him run out through the bifold doors to the garden before she crept up behind Kelly and hugged her around the waist, hooking her chin over her shoulder.

'You smell like...' she started.

'Get off me, you mad cow.' Kelly bumped her with her hip.

'I was going to say "gin and regret",' Cat said. 'But you actually smell gorgeous. What is that?'

'Zadig and Voltaire,' Kelly said, stirring some pasta shapes with a wooden spoon. Cat hadn't even seen her open the tin. 'Sean got it for me.'

'*Pfft*,' Cat said. 'I thought it was going to be sponcon.'

'This pasta's sponcon.' She gestured with the spoon.

'Seriously?'

Kelly laughed. 'No, dickhead.'

'I never know with you.'

When Cat first met Kelly she was just starting out as a blogger. Over the last few years, she'd become an incredibly popular and successful lifestyle blogger, appearing in ad campaigns for M&S and Asda, and being paid by brands for sponsored content on her blog. She earned more than Sean, but Cat was convinced she worked harder too. She didn't understand most of it, she had to admit, but occasionally Kelly got free mini breaks or spa sessions and took Cat along with her so she was one hundred per cent supportive and only a little bit jealous.

'Where is Sean?' Cat asked, reaching over and pinching a Wotsit from Arnold's Iron Man plate.

'Don't,' Kelly said. 'I'm ordering Thai.'

'I don't think one Wotsit's going to ruin my dinner. Shall I open the wine?' She was hoping Kelly would offer one of her own bottles, much better than the £8.99 stuff Cat had picked up in Londis, along with a bag of Kettle Chips and a family bar of Dairy Milk.

'Not until Arnold's in bed,' Kelly said.

'What? Why? Have you got gin then? He'll think it's pop.'

Kelly glanced back over her shoulder to make sure her son was still in the garden. 'He had to do a thing at school – like a picnic alphabet thing, right? He had to write and draw something for every letter of the alphabet. And do you know what he put for V?'

'Vagina?'

'Worse. Vodka.'

Cat snorted with laughter. 'Is that worse? I don't know.'

'Shut up. So I've stopped drinking in front of him. It's good for me anyway.'

'It's not good for me though. Why can't I drink? I don't mind his teacher thinking I'm a lush.'

'He's going to bed in about two hours. You can hang on till then.'

'Can I though?' Cat said.

While Kelly dished out Arnold's tea and called him in from the garden, Cat went to get her bag from the hall and retrieved the *Standard*. By the time she'd got to the shop, she'd regretted leaving it on the bench and picked up her own copy.

'Stop kicking,' Kelly said to Arnold as Cat walked back in.

'I wasn't,' Arnold mumbled.

Cat clambered up onto one of the bar stools and immediately drummed her feet against the side of the breakfast bar.

'Don't encourage him!' Kelly said. 'Let's see then.'

She flicked through the paper until she got to the Culture page. Cat studied her face as she read the short piece and then stared at the photo.

'He looks good,' she said eventually.

'I know,' Cat agreed.

'Did you google him?'

'Nah.'

Cat swiped another Wotsit. And she hadn't. She had looked him up on Facebook, however, while she'd been waiting for Kelly to turn up to collect her. But there hadn't been much to see there; his account was pretty locked down. Just the updated cover photos and profile pics, and there was nothing interesting there.

'Well done,' Kelly said.

'Did you see what his show's called?' Cat asked. It had been going round and round her head.

'Yeah.'

'What do you think?'

'I think it's an expression.'

'It is, yeah. But it's an expression with my name in it.'

Kelly sucked her bottom lip into her mouth. As far as Cat was aware, it was her only bad habit. And it made her look like a toddler. Cat loved it.

'I just don't think—' Kelly started.

'I know, I know.'

'It's been five years. Like, if he—'

'I mean, Taylor Swift's still writing songs about Harry Styles,' Cat said. 'Apparently. And that must be five years. And me and Sam were together longer than them. If they were even together in the first place. I saw this thing online about how it was a PR relationsh—'

'You can't go and see it,' Kelly interrupted.

Her lack of interest in celebrity gossip had always bugged Cat.

'I'm not going to!' Cat said. Even though that was exactly what she'd been planning to do.

'You can't. It'd be weird.'

'Would it though? Surely I'm allowed to take an interest. In an ex. I'd say it's healthy more than anything.'

'Who's Sam?' Arnold asked.

'My ex-boyfriend.'

Arnold tipped his head on one side while he thought. 'Did I ever met him?'

'Meet him,' Kelly automatically corrected.

'Nah,' Cat said. 'We split up before you were born.'

'See?' Kelly said. 'It's too long. An entire Arnold ago.'

'We're going to start measuring time in Arnolds now?' Cat said. 'Interesting. So I'm six Arnolds old?'

'How many am I?' Arnold asked.

Cat stared at him until he got it and they both laughed.

'You really shouldn't though,' Kelly said.

'But,' Cat said, pinching another Wotsit, 'consider this: what if I did?'

'He left,' Kelly said, giving her a hard stare.

'Everyone always leaves,' Cat said, faux-dramatically. 'You'll never leave me, will you, Arnold?'

'I'm going to Beavers tomorrow,' Arnold said, his eyes wide.

'You're breaking my heart,' Cat said, dropping another kiss to the top of his head.

'We'll talk about this later,' Kelly said.

'Can't wait.'

Cat met Kelly at university. Kelly had been a student and Cat had been going out with a boy, Justin, who was in one of Kelly's seminar groups. One afternoon, they'd all gone into the pub – Justin, Kelly, and a few of their student friends, and Cat, who kept avoiding questions about where she went to uni and what she was studying. It was one of those hot sunny days that just became dreamier and more relaxed the more they all drank. Plus the pub overlooked a canal, so Cat had managed to convince herself pretty early on that she was on holiday.

Kelly had been talking to one of the others for a while, but then she got up, took a couple of steps, and leaned down, her mouth close to Cat's ear. She said, 'I don't suppose you've got a tampon, have you?'

Cat was at first astonished – they were the first words Kelly had said to her beyond 'Hello'. She couldn't imagine a world where she asked a stranger for sanitary products – she'd be embarrassed to ask a friend – but then she was excited, because she did in fact have a tampon… she had a whole pack, unopened, that she'd bought that morning on the way to meet Justin.

She handed the entire packet over and watched in awe as Kelly walked into the bar with the Tampax in her hand; she didn't even hide them up her sleeve. She'd asked Kelly about it later – when they were madly in friend-love – and Kelly said people (mostly men) needed to get used to seeing tampons and not be freaked out by them. She said it was just a small thing, but she'd decided one day not to hide them and so she never did. She always had a pack out on the counter in the bathroom too. After a while, Cat did it as well (but she put them away if male friends came round, and then felt like a failure as a feminist).

Once Kelly had got back from the loo that day, she'd sat next to Cat and they'd talked and talked. The others from the seminar drifted away over the course of the evening, the sky darkened, fairy lights came on in the trees around the beer garden, music drifted out of the pub, but Kelly and Cat talked and talked. Justin tried to join in, but couldn't keep up with their conversation and eventually, exasperated, had announced he was leaving and asked if Cat was going with him or staying with Kelly.

She'd stayed with Kelly. And they'd been best friends ever since.

CHAPTER FOUR

Cat woke to watery sunlight through hot-pink curtains and stretched her arms and legs out as far as she could. Kelly's spare room was beautiful and had been at least partly designed with Cat in mind (and also for a feature on Kelly's blog). It both made Cat feel special (she had her own room in her best friend's house!) and like a loser (she had her own room in her best friend's house because her actual room in her own house was garbage).

At home she didn't get woken up by watery light through hot-pink curtains; she got woken up by the recycling being emptied in the pub at the back. Or by the guy upstairs having a wank. Or by her roommate Georgie having a row with her boyfriend. Here at Kelly's she always felt a bit like Audrey Hepburn in *Roman Holiday*. Her own home was more *Orange is the New Black*. Without the glamour.

She could smell coffee, which meant Sean was up. Coffee was one of Sean's responsibilities and he took it very seriously. Cat suddenly felt like she hadn't seen Sean for ages and she loved him a lot. Also, she wanted coffee. So she forced herself out of bed and straight down to the kitchen.

'Morning,' Sean said, glancing over his shoulder at her. He was already fully dressed in a navy suit with a pink shirt and brown leather shoes.

'You look hot,' Cat said, scratching her belly under the ancient Wallace & Gromit T-shirt she'd worn for bed.

Sean went pink, which was precisely why Cat had said it. Although he really did look hot.

'I've got a meeting in the Shard this morning.'

'Ooh, I love the Shard.' She sat at the breakfast island and picked a grape out of the huge wooden bowl in the middle. 'Someone on Facebook said it's worryingly phallic but I think if your penis looks like that—'

'Good morning!' Kelly said brightly, as she and Arnold joined them in the kitchen. 'Do we think that's appropriate breakfast conversation?'

'I don't see why not,' Cat said in an equally sing-song voice. 'Anatomy is educational.'

Unlike Sean, Kelly was still in her pyjamas – the pair Cat had bought her last Christmas with gnomes all over them and 'There's no place like gnome' on the bum – but looked a lot more awake than Cat felt. She kissed Sean on the cheek before joining Cat at the island. Arnold, also in pyjamas, hopped up next to Cat. Cat leaned over far enough to sniff his hair.

'Hmm,' she said. 'Sweet dreams with a hint of fart.'

'Cat!' Kelly said.

'What?'

'We have to say "trump",' Arnold said.

'Over my dead body,' Cat said.

Sean brought the coffee over and poured some for Cat in one of their pretty patterned over-sized teacups. Cat closed her eyes and inhaled the aroma. Usually she'd close her eyes and pretend she was in Paris, but she was more than happy where she was for once.

'Shouldn't you be getting ready for work?' Kelly said.

'Oh, you ruined it.' Cat opened her eyes and then narrowed them at her friend. 'Have you got something I can wear?'

'I already put it on your bed.'

Cat grinned. 'Thanks, Mum.'

'My mum,' Arnold muttered.

Cat raised one eyebrow at him. 'Sharing is caring, baby!'

'Touchy subject, I'm afraid,' Sean said. He was drinking his coffee black, even though Cat was convinced he didn't actually like it like that, but thought it made him seem more masculine.

'Why?' Cat sipped her coffee.

'Because in four months, Arnold's going to be a big brother.'

Cat choked on her coffee, coughed, and sprayed it across the table.

'Oh shit!' she croaked. 'Sorry. And sorry for the swear too. Don't say "shit", Arnold.'

'I won't,' Arnold said brightly.

Kelly wiped the table with kitchen roll and tore off a couple of sheets for Cat's face, while Sean grabbed her a bottle of water from the fridge. Something in Cat's chest felt like it was cracking, but she wasn't sure why.

'That is amazing news!' she said, hopping off her stool to squeeze Arnold and kiss the top of his head. 'You're going to be the best big brother.'

'I don't want a baby,' Arnold muttered.

'I don't blame you,' Cat told him. 'They're smelly and gross and cry a lot. The first time I met you I couldn't believe how horrible you were. But then you got bigger and cuter and funny and now you're amazing. Apart from the smell.'

Arnold smiled up at her and she kissed him on the nose, then rounded the table to hug Kelly.

'I can't believe you didn't tell me!' she said into her friend's glossy hair. 'How did you keep it secret?'

'I didn't mean to! I didn't realise for ages. And then we were waiting for scans and telling A and everything. I almost told you last night, but Sean wanted to see your face.'

'Aw, Sean,' Cat said, ruffling his hair.

'I need to get off,' Sean said, smoothing his hair with one hand and reaching for his wife's hand with the other.

'At the breakfast table?' Cat said. 'Even I wouldn't—'

'You're very funny,' he said, dipping his head to kiss Kelly. 'And we both know you would.'

'Sean!' Cat said, delighted.

His face was still bright red when he left the room.

'God, I love making him blush,' Cat said wistfully.

'You're awful,' Kelly said, clambering down off her own stool. 'We need to get sorted. I can drop you at Highgate Tube after I take Arnold, is that OK? Or will you be late?'

'Late probably. Again. But I don't care. That would be great.'

'You really shouldn't go to Sam's show, you know,' Kelly said in the car, once they'd dropped Arnold at school.

'I know,' Cat said. 'I just... what if it actually is about me.'

'Why would it be about you?'

'Why would it be called "Cat Among the Pigeons" if it's not about me?'

'I don't know.' Kelly frowned over the steering wheel. 'Maybe it's about pigeons.'

'You think it's more likely to be about pigeons than about me?'

'No? I don't know. I just don't want you to go and be disappointed.' She pulled into the right-hand lane and the car behind honked.

'So impatient,' Kelly muttered.

'Do you think I'll be disappointed if it is about me or if it isn't?' Cat asked.

Kelly glanced at her and then back at the road. 'I don't even know.'

Cat laughed. 'Me neither.' She stared out of the window for a while, looking at the enormous detached houses she'd never be able to buy, the restaurants she couldn't even afford to eat in.

'I just... I don't feel like I ever got any closure, you know? He left and that was it.'

'I know,' Kelly said, glancing over with a sympathetic smile.

Cat twisted her body so she was leaning back against the door and looking over at Kelly. 'Will you come with me?'

Kelly groaned. 'Oh god. I suppose so.'

'This is why you're my best friend.'

'I know,' Kelly said. 'It's a nightmare.'

Colin was out of the office, and a few phone calls brought Cat up to date on her live cases. She had a note in her diary to follow up with some previous clients – see if they had any new business – but she could do that after lunch.

Instead she angled her computer screen towards the wall, shifted her chair slightly, and googled Sam. It was unlikely that anyone would notice or even care, but she didn't want anyone else knowing her business. Particularly when it involved Sam.

She went to Images first and scrolled down the page. There was the photo from the paper and other photos from other shows. He was definitely doing better than she'd realised, but she didn't go to comedy clubs any more, hadn't for five years, not since she'd stopped doing stand-up herself. There was a photo of him with his arm round a woman, but after staring at it for a few seconds, Cat decided it was a fan. God. Sam had fans. There were photos of him backstage with other comedians, even one of him sitting on a sofa chatting with Gemma Jewell, Cat's absolute favourite. What if he was going out with Gemma Jewell? That would be a nightmare. Although she couldn't begrudge him; talk about an upgrade. In another tab, Cat googled Gemma Jewell and found she was apparently totally loved up with her high school sweetheart, so maybe they were just friends. Cat hoped not even. She hoped Sam had just sat there for the photo and then buggered off.

A bit more scrolling and she saw a photo that made her catch her breath. She knew that photo like she knew her own reflection. It had been the lock screen on her phone. She'd taken it in the pub after one of Sam's earliest stand-up gigs. He'd only done a couple of minutes and he'd been so nervous beforehand that he'd vomited in the street. But he'd nailed it. And then they'd all got hammered. She smiled at her unintentional mental pun.

Sam was smiling directly into the camera and it wasn't the best photo of him she'd ever taken – he'd had his hair cut that day and it was too short and all standing on end like a loo brush – but he looked so happy and tired and relieved. And she'd been so proud of him. She could barely wait for him to get down from the makeshift stage and back over to their table so she could wrap her arms around him and press her face into his neck and tell him how brilliant he'd been. And there it was. There he was. Her photo. In Google image search.

She clicked through to the article. It was a piece about an Australian comedy festival. Of course it was. Sam had flown over for it for the first time while they were still together and Cat had been incredibly envious, but also incredibly proud. She'd wanted to go with him – he'd asked her to – but she couldn't afford it. His parents had paid for him and they'd offered to pay for Cat too, but she'd said no, it was too much. His mum had cornered her in their kitchen one evening and tried to convince her, saying that they'd be delighted to since Cat didn't have any parents of her own, well, her dad, but—

And Cat had spluttered a few excuses and legged it. She'd hated being rude to Jan, who had always been lovely, but there was just no way. So Sam had gone to the Melbourne International Comedy Festival and Cat had gone to stay with Kelly and sulk until he came back. But when he'd got back, he'd been full of talk about promoters and how much opportunity there was out there and how he could get so many more gigs, and – eventually – how he was thinking about moving out there, at least for a year or so, and how his parents supported the idea and what did Cat think?

And she'd waited for him to ask her to go with her. She'd waited for him to talk about it being a great opportunity for Cat too. But he never did. And then he left. And that had been that.

CHAPTER FIVE

Cat had met Sam when he ran her over on his bike. She'd been on a date that had been a total disaster. The guy had spent most of the evening looking at his phone and had seemed annoyed with Cat for expecting him to make conversation. She'd spent almost an hour trying to come up with an excuse to leave, and eventually she'd just said, 'Sorry, I've got to go' and walked out. She'd walked along the Embankment, looking out over the water and the bridges and the Houses of Parliament, and thinking about how much she loved London at times like that, but how few times like that she actually had. And then she'd looked the wrong way before crossing the road and Sam had hit her with his bike.

One minute she'd been taking a step and looking up at a beautiful white building with curved stone across the top, wondering if it was a government building or something more interesting, and the next she was on her arse with pain radiating up her hips and a really hot man looking down at her. He was full of apologies, even though it had been entirely her fault and she was embarrassed. Plus she'd dropped her bag and everything had rolled out of it including tampons and condoms and she was embarrassed about that even though she knew she shouldn't be because they were both sensible things for a twenty-two-year-old woman to carry. She'd tried to be more Kelly, but she still wasn't quite there. Also she'd smashed her phone.

The hot man helped her to her feet and off the road and onto the pavement alongside the river. She sat on a bench and checked herself for injury while the hot man – who had, by this time, introduced himself as Sam, but who Cat was still calling 'the hot man' in her head – asked if she wanted him to take her to hospital. She eventually convinced him that she didn't need hospital but she would quite like a drink and so they walked to a pub on Villiers Street and Sam bought her a brandy because he said it was good for shock. She'd never had brandy before and it made her head feel heavy, but she still ordered a lager after because she didn't want to leave.

Despite having hit her with his bike (yes, even though it was her fault), Sam seemed nice. And funny. And hot. He asked where she'd been and she told him about the disastrous date and he said the guy must've been an idiot to be more interested in his phone than in Cat. And then he took a gulp of his beer and then looked at his own phone, but he hadn't been joking or taking the piss and when he realised what he'd done, they both laughed and Cat thought, I could like you.

Cat was halfway through her pint when he asked her what she did for a living and she told him about the boring office job she'd taken just to pay the bills while she tried to become a stand-up comedian. And he said, 'Are you shitting me?' and she said no. Which was when he told her he was also a stand-up comedian, pretty much just starting out, although it transpired that he was a bit further along than Cat was. And they laughed about what a massive coincidence it was and then argued about which of them got to put the story of how they met into their routines.

They'd both ended up doing it and it had worked for both of them. In fact, quite often they'd both work aspects of their relationship into their respective stand-up routines and Cat had loved it. It had sort of been like therapy, seeing things from the other person's perspective, but with the addition of their own and the audience's laughter. They'd even talked about doing a sort of 'He said/she said' joint show, but had never got further than talking about it.

So Cat felt like she couldn't really be pissed off that Sam was still doing stand-up about her when she was the one who'd stopped.

'It's cos you've got no, like, right to reply,' Kelly said when Cat phoned her. Kelly had been throwing up so Sean had come home from work early and collected Arnold so Kelly could go back to bed.

'I guess,' Cat said. But she didn't think it was that.

'Like in the past you could've responded to this. Either onstage or actually to him, you know, in your actual life. But now you just have to accept it.'

'Maybe,' Cat said. And she thought there was perhaps a little truth in it but she was sure there was something else too, a niggling feeling in her stomach that she couldn't quite identify.

'I know he has the right to talk about his life,' Cat said. 'But it's my life he's talking about too.'

'Maybe,' Kelly said.

Cat ignored her. 'And he's used my name. I think that's it. It's cos my name's in it. So people will know it's about me.'

'If it is about you. We don't even know yet. And I think if it really bothered you, you could ask him to not? Wasn't there a stand-up recently whose ex sued her?'

'God,' Cat said. 'Imagine. I don't want to do that.'

'Of course you don't.'

There was something in Kelly's tone that made Cat think she knew something Cat didn't.

'What?' she said, rotating her office chair slowly to make sure no one was sneaking up on her or listening to her conversation.

'What?' Kelly echoed.

'What are you thinking?'

She heard Kelly suck in a breath. 'You know. You know what's bothering you about it. You just can't admit it to yourself. Denial—'

'Not just a member of One Direction, I know. You think I'm feeling guilty?'

'You're always feeling guilty.'

'You think I should have asked to go with him.'

'I think you could have done, yeah.'

'You don't think it was up to him to ask me? He was the one moving away. It wouldn't have been normal to say, hey, I'm moving to the other side of the world, would you fancy coming with me? Or even, long distance isn't so bad these days with Skype sex and whatnot?'

'I think he should have asked, yeah. But I also think you could have asked. And we both know why you didn't.'

'This isn't about my dad.'

'Isn't it?' Kelly said.

'You're really annoying,' Cat said.

'Look, we don't even know if it's actually about you. Let's wait and see it before we rain hellfire upon him.'

'Obviously it is about me,' Cat said.

'We'll see.'

Cat woke in the middle of the night, stomach churning. At first, she couldn't place the source of her anxiety and then she remembered: Sam's show.

She just wouldn't go, she decided. She didn't need to. Just because he was back didn't mean she had to seek him out. She could just pretend he was still in Australia. *But.* If the show *was* about her, she really should go and see it. She wanted to know what he was saying. What if it was about how he never should have left, had regretted it every day, crying himself to sleep and… Yeah, it wasn't going to be that.

But what if it was about why he'd left? Why he hadn't asked Cat to go with him? What if it answered all the questions she'd been asking herself for the past five years? She had to go then. It would be ridiculous not to.

CHAPTER SIX

It wasn't a huge venue. It wasn't The Comedy Club or Jongleurs. It was one of the smaller rooms in a multi-space venue, but the bar was buzzing and it made Cat's stomach flutter. She'd side-eyed Sam's poster – with its glowing testimonials from other comedians – on the way in. She'd read them all online by now anyway. And since she was about to see his actual face in real life, she didn't need to look at yet another photo.

'Beer?' Kelly asked.

'What are you having?'

'J2O probably.'

'Christ. Yeah, I'll have a beer please.' She should've asked Kelly to get her two. At least. Since she did not want to do this sober. Actually she should've gone to the bar, not Kelly, because Kelly was pregnant and—

Harvey. Harvey was there. She'd been so focused on Sam, that she hadn't even thought about whoever else might be there. If he saw her, he'd tell Sam and she didn't want Sam to know she was there because then Sam would think... she didn't even know what Sam would think because she had to get away from his brother. She pushed through the small crowd – she'd have to text Kelly once she was safely hidden – and through the double doors out to the foyer. People were still coming in, chatting and laughing. It was a pretty young crowd and slightly more hipster than Cat had been expecting. She excused herself all the way to the exterior doors and stepped out onto the street. It was bloody freezing and her coat was inside.

'Shit.' She texted Kelly to say she'd just nipped out and then looked around. The only other people standing out in the cold were smokers. She really should have started smoking years ago, for moments just like this.

'Sorry,' she said to the nearest man – a skinny guy with a floppy fringe and a worried expression, like a guinea pig, 'I couldn't bum one, could I? I've just had a bit of a shock.'

He rolled his eyes, but he handed her a cigarette and lit it for her. She thanked him, put it in her mouth and turned away so he wouldn't see her not actually inhaling. And she did feel like she'd had a bit of a shock. She hadn't thought about Sam's family. She'd made herself not think about Sam's family. Because they'd been so bloody lovely. It had been almost as hard losing them as it had him. And Harvey had looked so good. He was younger than Sam and he'd been maybe twenty when they'd split. And even though he'd been handsome then, he'd been handsome like a teenager – gawky and not quite in control of his limbs. But the man she'd seen in the bar hadn't been like that at all. He'd been—

'So when did you start smoking?' Harvey said directly into her ear.

She inhaled sharply, setting off a coughing fit that made her eyes stream and flecks of saliva fly out of her mouth. She half hoped she'd actually die since when she stopped coughing she'd have to explain why she'd been outside in the freezing cold pretending to smoke in order to avoid her ex-boyfriend's brother.

'I, um, don't. Much,' she managed to croak out.

'Really? You seem so comfortable with it?' He grinned at her, the corners of his eyes crinkling.

'Fuck,' she said. 'It's really good to see you.'

He ducked down and wrapped his arms around her, pulling her into a tight hug.

'Are you actually taller?' she said into his shoulder. 'Or have I just forgotten how tall you were?'

'I don't think I'm taller,' he said, releasing her. 'Pretty sure I was fully grown last time we saw each other. Does Sam know you're here?'

'Fuck no!'

Harvey laughed. 'I assumed. So that's why you legged it when you saw me?'

'I did not "leg it",' Cat said, blinking; the cigarette smoke was curling up and burning her eyes. 'I came outside for a… break.'

'Right.' Harvey reached over and took the cig out of her fingers and put it in his mouth, sucking on it until his cheeks hollowed. He blew out a couple of smoke rings, dropped the cigarette on the floor and crushed it with his foot. Cat stared at him. It was, no question, one of the hottest things she'd ever seen. She was furious with herself.

'I don't think you should see the show,' he said, a frown line appearing between his eyebrows.

'I'm pretty sure you remember me well enough to know that I am one hundred per cent going to go, now that you've said that.'

Harvey sighed. 'Yeah. I mean, I didn't remember that. But now I do.'

'It's about me, right?'

Harvey bit his bottom lip and dropped his head back, looking up at the sky. Cat stared at his jawline, which was, quite frankly, completely ridiculous.

'It's not about you exactly. But there's a lot about you in it.'

'Is he shitty about me?'

'No?' Harvey said.

Cat barked out a laugh. It hurt the back of her throat. Stupid bloody cigarette. 'Is it good?'

'Yeah. It's really good.' He had the decency to look apologetic.

'I want to see it then. Come on. I left Kelly in the bar.'

*

'It's not too late to back out,' Kelly whispered, as the lights went down in the theatre. When Cat and Harvey had got back to the bar, Kelly had been chatting and laughing with a woman who apparently followed her blog and was a PR for a nearby hotel. So no doubt Kelly and Sean would soon be off for some sort of saucy mini-break gratis. Her life, honestly.

'It really is,' Cat whispered back. 'For a start, it'd be dead obvious if we left now. And of course I have to see it, now I know for sure.'

'OK,' Kelly said. 'Well. If it's horrible or mean we can leave at any time. I can cause a diversion.'

'It's way too soon for you to fake labour; you're hardly even showing.'

And then Sam walked out onto the stage. No fanfare or fireworks, just a man strolling out from behind the curtain. Cat still found it hard to breathe. Kelly grabbed her hand and squeezed it.

'When I was a kid,' Sam said, 'I was desperate for a pet. I didn't care what it was. I just wanted something to love unconditionally. Something I could cuddle at night. Something that would be happy to see me when I got home from school. So my mum got me a cat.'

Big laugh. Cat slumped down a little in her seat while Sam talked about how at first the cat – Sparky – had been affectionate and sweet, but how, over time, it had become withholding and emotionless.

Cat wanted to leave. She knew exactly where the story was going and, while it was pretty much what she'd expected, it turned out she didn't want to hear it after all. Not in front of Kelly. Not in front of Harvey. But of course she couldn't leave. Not when he would see her go.

Sam was confident, poised, more comfortable onstage than he had been when they were together. His timing was better. He got bigger laughs. As he moved on from the original cat/Cat comparison to talking about the girlfriend he was with after Cat, she sat back up in her seat again. She didn't really want to hear about her, whoever she was, but she was fascinated watching Sam again.

'He's really good,' Kelly whispered about ten minutes in and Cat just nodded. He really was.

He talked about Cat – not by name, just as one of his exes. The show was about his various previous girlfriends and the mistakes he'd made with them. Cat had been transfixed, leaning forward in her seat so she didn't miss a word. He was charming and sexy and still did the thing he used to do where he started to laugh during a story as if there was just no way it wasn't hilarious. Often the audience was laughing with him before he even got to the punchline.

He compared his relationships to animals, talking about Old Cow/New Cow theory, which Cat had remembered them talking about years ago when they saw it in a film. It suggests that once a bull has mated with an old cow, he wants a new cow for any future mating opportunities. Sam said that had never been his experience. He was more of a sloth, in that once he was settled in a relationship he relaxed so much that it was almost indistinguishable from letting himself go and not giving a shit.

The title came from a bit he did about a cat he'd seen stalking a pigeon on a wall. It had spent ages creeping carefully closer – its eyes bright with want – and then it pounced and caught the pigeon and didn't know what to do with it. It held the terrified, fluttering bird between its front paws for a minute and then let go, watching in bewilderment as it flew away.

'So he thinks I chased him and caught him and then didn't know what to do with him?' Cat said, once they were out on the street and walking back to the car.

'God,' Kelly said, glancing around as if she couldn't quite remember where they'd parked, 'I don't know. I don't think so. I think, if anything, you're the pigeon.'

Cat rolled her eyes. 'How can I be the pigeon? I didn't fly away. He flew all the way to Australia. Can pigeons even do that? Maybe he's, I don't know, a goose?'

'I didn't buy most of the analogies.' Kelly seemed to decide left was the correct direction and set off. Cat couldn't remember where they'd parked either, so she just followed. 'I mean, he was funny. But it wouldn't hold up, like, scientifically.'

'Sean didn't want a new cow after you had Arnold, did he,' Cat said.

Kelly snorted. 'No way.'

'And he won't after the next one either.'

'No.' Kelly said. 'He'd better not.'

'Did you see Harvey?' Cat said.

Kelly stopped walking and turned to stare at her. 'Fuck! Yeah, I was going to say. Bloody hell, he looked hot!'

Cat scoffed. 'That's your pregnancy hormones talking.'

'Nope. He was always really cute, but my god, I felt my knickers vibrate.'

'I'm telling Sean,' Cat said. 'I'm texting him now.' She didn't even have her phone out.

'Did you talk to him?' Kelly asked. She'd stopped at another junction and was looking left to right.

'Do you really not know where we parked?'

'It was somewhere around here. Did you?'

'What?'

'Talk to him.'

'Harvey? Yeah. A bit. After I saw him and ran away and went outside and pretended to smoke and then he came out and called me out on it. I was totally chill.'

'How do you get yourself into these situations?' Kelly asked.

'I don't know,' Cat said. 'But you're the one who can't find your car.'

CHAPTER SEVEN

Cat had a meeting with a new client and then a VAT Return to finalise and then she was pretty much done, beyond all the fiddly little things she kept putting off because they were just too boring. Colin's office door was closed and everyone else was either out or heads-down busy. When Cat had first started, she'd offer to help other account managers when her own work was done, but everyone kept ownership of their own projects and so it just didn't work that way. When she was done she was done. And she was good at her job, so she often found herself at a loose end. It reminded her of school when she always used to finish exams before everyone else and would then sit there, wondering if she'd missed something vital. But no, she was just fast.

So for the past hour or so, she'd been idly wandering around the internet. And she hadn't even googled Sam once. OK, once. But she made herself click away before the page loaded.

She made herself a cup of tea and nicked a KitKat out of Phil's drawer, before opening Facebook and typing in Sam's mum's name. She'd promised Kelly she wouldn't google Sam, she'd promised herself she wouldn't search for Harvey – she'd said nothing about their mum. So she wasn't doing anything wrong. She scrolled down Jan's timeline pretending to be interested in the Christmas shopping day she'd had at Brent Cross or the new boots she'd bought, while the rest of her brain was screaming at her to click on Sam's page.

Instead she came to a photo of Jan and Harvey. They were standing in the middle of a white room with big windows down one side. Harvey had his arm around Jan's shoulders – he was at least a foot taller than her – and her arm was curled around his waist. They were both beaming into the camera.

The photo was captioned '#proudmama'.

Harvey was tagged in the photo, so Cat clicked on the link to his page while shoving the last two KitKat fingers in her mouth. That wasn't googling. She was just clicking on a link. She clicked on links all the time; it was no big deal.

'Holy shit,' she whispered, as his page loaded.

His profile photo showed him in a grey hoodie, hood up, but he also had sunglasses pushed up on his forehead, holding his messy hair back. His forehead was furrowed and he was looking into the camera as if to say 'What?' There was a view of London in the background, so it had obviously been taken on a rooftop somewhere. Cat studied the dimples at the corners of his mouth, the hint of scruff on his upper lip. The small mole on his jaw, his one slightly arched eyebrow.

'Boyfriend?' a voice said from behind her and she jumped, clicking away from the page. Unfortunately, the next open tab was a Google Image search for 'The Rock shirtless', which was arguably worse. She minimised the whole thing.

'Yeah,' she said, turning in her chair to smile up at Nick. 'Back again?'

Nick had definitely been turning up more often since he'd told them about New York. Cat assumed he was tying up some loose ends.

'I was just passing. Thought I'd pop in. You've got a bit of...' He reached out towards her face and she didn't know what to do. She stared at his hand coming closer, until his thumb brushed the corner of her mouth. 'Chocolate?' he said.

'KitKat,' she croaked. 'Ta.'

He smiled. 'Are you busy?'

Cat forced herself not to look at her screen. 'Not so much actually. Why?'

'I was wondering if you could run me through your cases. I want to make sure I'm up to date on everything before I, you know, bugger off.'

'That's fine,' Cat said, sliding her drawer open and pulling out her live account folder. 'Still can't believe you're doing that, by the way.'

'I know,' Nick said. 'I'm a monster. Do you want to do it here or in the conference room?'

A vision of exactly what she'd like to do to Nick in the conference room flickered through her mind. And it wasn't anything to do with accountancy.

Cat shook her head to try to clear her thoughts. She'd attempted to fantasise about Nick more than once, but she was terrible at it. Once she'd come up with this elaborate scenario of her working late (would never happen) and him dropping by to pick something up (unlikely) and bending her over her desk. But then Colin had walked in and asked if Cat had done the filing and then just stood there, arms folded, shirt buttoned up wrong, while Nick humped away and Cat tried to answer some emails. Pitiful.

'Conference room,' she said. And hoped she wasn't blushing. The way Nick was smiling at her suggested that might have been a vain hope.

Cat followed Nick to the conference room, watching his long legs in black trousers, tight around his arse. That probably constituted inappropriate workplace behaviour actually. She should probably stop.

In the conference room, Nick opened the windows overlooking the square.

'It's hot in here,' he told her, as she watched the way his shoulders pulled at the fabric of his shirt.

So take off all your clothes, Cat thought, and then immediately tried to think of another song to chase away the earworm. She did not want to idly start singing that as she showed Nick the spreadsheets.

(Spreadsheets? Since when was accountancy so full of innuendo?)

'I just need to pop to the loo,' Cat told Nick, pushing her chair back and heading for the door. 'Feel free to start without me.'

'Oh my GOD,' she muttered, as she fast-walked to the bathrooms.

Nick's here, she texted Kelly, as soon as she was locked in a cubicle.

Three dots appeared immediately. *Phwoar.*

He's wearing tight black trousers.

Kelly sent back an unseemly amount of aubergine emojis.

He touched my mouth. I had chocolate on my face.

A row of alternating tongue and blushy faces.

Pregnancy hormones? Cat texted.

Kelly replied with a row of water splashes.

And, to be fair to Kelly, she'd been thirsty for Nick before she got pregnant, first via Facebook stalking and then after meeting him in a bar when she'd come to pick Cat up after work.

Cat gave up on texting and called. 'Everything I say sounds like an innuendo,' she said, as soon as Kelly picked up.

'You know why that is.'

'Because he's hot.'

'Because he's hot and you haven't had sex for, like, ever.'

'I can't sleep with Nick.'

'Why not?'

'I work with him. I mean, I work *for* him.'

'Ah, but he's leaving.'

'The country, not the company. He'd still be my superior.'

'That could be hot,' Kelly said.

'Oh my god. That is not going to happen.'

'I'm just saying it could. If you wanted. And I think it would be good. For you. And also for me when you gave me all the details. Tell me more about his trousers.'

'Never mind his trousers. He asked me if Harvey was my boyfriend. And I said yes.'

'What? Why would you say that?'

'He surprised me. Came up behind me.'

'Imagine I'm sending you many aubergine emojis right now.'

'I'm starting to think you're the one who needs to get laid.'

'You're not wrong. You still OK to take Arnold to the grotto on Sunday?'

'Yeah,' she said. 'I'm looking forward to it.'

It was actually the only thing she was looking forward to. Which was pretty bloody sad.

'I'd better go. Don't want him to think I'm pooing.'

After ending the call, Cat splashed cold water on her face, pulled her hair out of its haphazard ponytail and put on lipstick. And then blotted it off again because what the fuck was she thinking. Nick had seen her with melted KitKat round her mouth earlier; the mystery was already gone. And she wasn't going to sleep with him anyway. Of course she wasn't. They were colleagues. And that was all they'd ever be.

Cat could hear the TV from the stairwell. Which meant that Georgie and her boyfriend were both home. Great. She pushed open the door and thought about going straight to her room, but her stomach was rumbling and she wanted the beer she knew she had in the fridge so she crossed the living room, calling out, 'Hiya!' as she went.

Something caught her eye and she stopped and looked over. Pete was lying on the floor and Georgie was sitting on his back.

'What are you doing?' she asked, before she could think better of it. They both appeared to be dressed, at least. The coffee table was covered in take-out containers and empty bottles.

'Cracking his neck,' Georgie said.

'You should let her do yours,' Pete said. His voice sounded strained. 'I've often thought you hold a lot of tension in your neck.'

'I don't,' Cat said, even though she did. 'How do you know how to do that?'

'YouTube,' Georgie said, leaning forward and sliding her hands down the side of Pete's neck. 'You can learn literally anything on YouTube. Just relax.'

'You're doing it again?' Cat asked.

'Love the sound it makes,' Georgie said.

'And it feels really good,' Pete added.

Cat's stomach lurched. She didn't want to hear it. Didn't want to see it. Was half convinced Georgie was about to snap Pete's head clean off.

'Could you just wait till I'm in my room?' Cat said. 'I'm squeamish about things like—'

There was a crack like a gunshot and then Pete groaned in relief.

'Oh my god,' Cat muttered, almost scurrying to the kitchen. 'I need to move.'

While her burrito was reheating, she ignored the dirty dishes piled up in the sink, the overflowing bin, the puddle of what she hoped was water on the counter, and instead opened the fridge to get her beer. More takeaway containers. A massive brick of cheese. A plastic tub of mini pork pies that Pete snacked on constantly. But no beer.

'Have you seen my beer?' she called out, pointlessly.

'Oh yeah,' Pete yelled back. 'Sorry. Didn't know it was yours.'

'Who else's could it have been,' Cat said under her breath. She poured herself a glass of water, got her burrito out of the microwave, and headed back to her room.

While she ate her burrito, the sauce running down her arms, she tortured herself by looking for flats she could never afford. The first one she found – a one-bedroom in Highbury Hill – cost more than her month's pay. A 'wonderfully spacious maisonette' in Shepherd's Bush cost almost five grand a month, with its 'pretty decked garden' and 'wood flooring throughout'. Cat didn't need a garden, pretty, decked or otherwise, or wood flooring; she just needed somewhere where no one drank her beer or cracked each other's necks in front of the TV.

She gave up on the unrealistic propositions and typed her maximum rent budget into the box. The screen transformed from bright open spaces to poky dark rooms in which the single beds touched both walls and offered a microwave as a headboard in houses of 'multiple occupation'.

One of them showed a plain beige room with metal-framed bunk beds in the centre, and no other furniture at all. Another was an attic conversion that Cat knew she wouldn't even be able to stand up in. She shut her laptop and lay back on the bed, staring up at the ceiling. She should be doing better by now; she knew it. She couldn't understand why she wasn't. How was Kelly married, with a child and another one on the way, living in a beautiful (huge) house with a hot husband and Cat was stuck in a poky room, working a job that bored her, and hadn't even had sex for bloody years.

Maybe she should ask Kelly if she could go and stay with her for a bit. Help out with the baby. Save some money for a better flat. Except last time Cat had lived with Kelly, Kelly had chucked her out and they'd had one of the worst rows of their friendship. Maybe she should look for another job. Particularly since Nick was leaving. She should definitely look for a different job. But tomorrow. Looking at flats had already depressed her; she didn't need to be made to feel worse. She sat back up and opened her laptop.

She'd finish her burrito, have a shower, a wank and an early night. That's what she'd do.

But first, she'd just have another little look at Harvey's Facebook.

CHAPTER EIGHT

'Woah,' Cat said, as she pushed open the door and let Arnold walk under her arm. 'I didn't think it would be this busy.'

It was a Saturday a few weeks before Christmas, so of course the department store was absolutely heaving. People were scuttling in every direction and Cat couldn't even see the best way to head or any signs for Santa's Grotto.

'You keep tight hold of my hand,' she told Arnold. 'I don't want to get lost.'

'I don't want to get lost!' Arnold said, gripping her hand with his tiny starfish one.

'Oh, you'd be fine,' Cat told him, giving his fingers a quick squeeze. 'But I'd totally cry. Anyway, if you got lost, I'd be able to find you by scent.'

She dipped down, pressed her nose against his hair, and sniffed. 'Glitter. And reindeer bums.'

As Arnold giggled, Cat spotted a gap in the crowds and headed in, tugging Arnold along with her.

'It's on the top floor, apparently,' she told him. 'So we either have to get the escalators or the lift. Which do you prefer?'

'Escalator!' Arnold yelled, hopping a little.

'OK, calm down; they're just moving stairs.'

Cat craned her neck until she spotted a sign and they headed towards it, dodging people walking the opposite direction and hoping it was a little less jam-packed upstairs. They joined the queue for the escalator and Cat pulled Arnold a little closer, as shoppers bumped into them from both sides.

'This is nuts,' Cat muttered. 'Why are we even here?'

'To see Santa!' Arnold yelled.

'Oh yeah, that's right.'

They shuffled to the bottom of the escalator and Cat stepped onto it, but Arnold, still holding her hand, had stopped dead. Cat's right leg, still on the escalator, stretched away from her.

'Shit!' she said, clinging to the handrail with her right hand, while trying to keep hold of Arnold with the other.

'Arnold!' she called back over her shoulder. 'Can you step on? I—' She tried to pull her leg back down, but she couldn't move it. 'Shit shit shit,' she chanted as she felt Arnold's hand slipping out of hers.

The whole thing felt like it was happening in slow motion, but also too quickly for her to have time to think. Her other leg buckled and she fell to her knees on the escalator, which was, of course, still going up. She tried to turn back and check on Arnold and managed a glimpse of his worried face before she was at the top and someone was helping her to her feet.

'Are you OK?' someone said.

'I need to get down to my little boy,' Cat said.

'Someone can bring him up,' a woman said.

'No, he won't. That's why I—' Cat shook her head. 'Where's the down one?'

'Right here.'

Someone guided her to the down escalator and held her arm as she stepped on, and continued holding her arm all the way back down. Cat couldn't even think or look or focus on anything other than getting back down to Arnold. She'd heard about tunnel vision, but she'd never experienced it before.

'That was so cool!' Arnold said, grabbing Cat around the thighs.

'It bloody wasn't,' Cat said, leaning down to cuddle him and sniffing just behind his ear. 'I nearly did the splits!'

'I got scared,' Arnold said, looking up at her with big eyes.

'Yeah, I worked that out, mate.'

Now that she knew Arnold was safe and OK, she relaxed enough to look around and found that she was quite the centre of attention.

'Thank you!' she called out. 'I'm fine!'

'You should go and get a cup of tea,' the woman who'd brought her down from upstairs said.

Cat turned to look at her for the first time. She had short dark hair, bright-red lipstick and a tattoo of a crystal heart on her chest. Cat would have been scared to speak to her under normal circumstances. 'Or something stronger.'

Cat smiled. 'Thanks for helping.'

'No problem. But seriously, you probably feel fine now because of the adrenaline, but you're gonna feel like shit later.' She glanced down at Arnold and mouthed, 'Sorry.'

'Cat said that when she fell down,' Arnold told her.

Cat rolled her eyes. 'Yes, I did. But that wasn't very nice of me, was it? It was just cos I was scared. So you're not going to repeat it, are you?'

Arnold grinned up at her and the woman with the heart tattoo smiled at them both.

Cat thanked the people who'd taken care of Arnold. She got the distinct impression that quite a few people had hung around just to see what Cat was going to do, but she thanked them anyway. And then she and Arnold went to find the lift.

'I think I need to sit down and get a cup of tea before we go and see Father Christmas,' Cat told Arnold, once they were in the lift. 'Is that OK with you? Sorry you have to wait.'

'Can I have cake?' Arnold asked.

'I like the way you think.'

'Woah,' Arnold said as they walked inside and saw a table completely covered with desserts. Cupcakes, scones, macarons, brownies, meringues, even a gingerbread person under a bell jar. Arnold's eyes were wide and bright.

'Get whatever you want, babe,' Cat said. She reached for a meringue for herself, figuring she needed the sugar. Arnold couldn't seem to decide between a cupcake, a brownie and the gingerbread person. While he was deciding, Cat looked across the cafe to see where they'd like to sit and saw Harvey.

Of course. Why not? He was sitting next to the window, the diffuse light shining over his face as he dipped his head to look at his phone. Cat checked out the rest of the room. If, once Arnold had chosen a cake, they walked straight over to the counter for drinks and then sat at the far side of the room and Cat kept her back to—

'Cat?'

Shit.

'Oh hi!' she said, turning and smiling. Except she said it before she turned, so totally failed at the pretending-she-hadn't-seen-him-already. Harvey grinned at her, the dimple in his cheek popping.

'Can I get two?' Arnold said.

Cat looked down to see he had a brownie in one hand and the gingerbread person in the other.

'Well, you're going to have to now, aren't you? They're meant to go on plates!'

Arnold grinned at her and she suspected he'd known exactly what he was doing.

'Hi!' Harvey said, his voice sounding slightly strained. 'I'm Harvey.'

'God,' Cat said. 'Sorry. Arnold, Harvey. Harvey, Arnold.'

Harvey had an expression on his face that Cat couldn't quite identify. 'We're going to go and get drinks,' Cat said. 'Do you want anything?'

'Actually,' Harvey said, 'I need to get back to work.'

'Yeah?' Cat said. 'You work near here, right?'

Shit. She'd got that off Facebook.

'How do you know that?' Harvey asked.

He was doing the dimple-grin thing again, like he knew exactly how many times she'd been on his Facebook. Oh god, maybe he did. Was there some sort of app that showed you how many times someone looked at your profile? There was on LinkedIn, which Cat had only learned after looking at Nick's page every day for a week (she'd told Nick it had been for work reasons when it had actually been for how hot he looked in his profile pic reasons).

'Can't remember,' Cat said. 'Someone mentioned it...'

He was still grinning at her. It made her stomach feel weird.

'Do you need to get back right now?' Cat said. 'Or can you join us for a cake? I'm sure Arnold wouldn't mind getting his grubby paws on another one for you.'

Harvey looked down at Arnold and then at his phone.

'Yeah. Actually. I can stay for a bit. Want to grab a cupcake for me, Arnold?'

'On a plate!' Cat said.

Cat didn't think she'd ever seen Harvey interacting with a child before. She thought she'd probably remember if she had because he was so bloody cute. He was totally relaxed chatting to Arnold and asking him interesting things rather than the usual 'Do you like *school*?', 'Have you got a *girlfriend*?' nonsense. And Arnold was looking at Harvey like he'd looked at the cakes, all wide-eyed and love-struck.

'So how's things with you?' Cat asked Harvey, once he'd finished doing an impersonation of a pirate that had Arnold in stitches. Cat had missed the inspiration for it, too busy trying to think of a way to have a normal conversation with Harvey.

'Good,' Harvey said. 'Thanks. Great actually. You? You still working at...'

'Yeah. Sort of.' How she wished she could say no. 'We merged with another company, but basically, yeah. For now, at least. It's secure, you know.' Shut up, Cat. 'Which is important.' She was more than aware that Harvey was likely to tell Sam he'd seen her. And Sam would ask what she was up to. And she hated the idea that Harvey would say, oh, the same. 'Particularly cos I'm doing stand-up again,' she said. SHUT UP, CAT.

'You are?' Harvey said, his eyebrows flicking upwards.

Cat nodded, biting her lip. There was no way out of it. She couldn't say, 'Oh, did I say stand-up? I meant to say cos I'm doing Zumba again... how funny.' She coughed. 'It's early days, but... yeah.'

'God,' Harvey said. 'That's great. I remember you were really good.'

Cat nodded. 'Thanks, yeah. I mean... I don't know about that.'

'No, you were. I always thought it was a shame that...' He glanced at Arnold, who was very industriously biting the legs off his gingerbread person. 'That you stopped. When... you know.'

When Sam left you and fucked off to Australia, Cat filled in. In her head.

'Yeah, it just wasn't the right time,' she told Harvey. 'Now's better.'

'Well, that's really good,' Harvey said. 'I'm proud of you.'

Cat felt that cracking in her chest again and for a second she had to swallow hard, digging her fingernails into her thighs, so she didn't cry. 'Proud of you' was her kryptonite. She picked up her brownie and took an enormous bite.

'I'd really better get back,' Harvey said then, pushing his chair back and standing. He was so tall. Taller than Sam. Cat gave him a tight-lipped smile, since she was worried about having brownie on her teeth. She wiped her mouth quickly, the memory of Nick and the KitKat still fresh.

'Been really good to meet you,' Harvey told Arnold.

Arnold gazed up at him.

'The pantomime starts next week,' Harvey told Cat. 'I could get you tickets? If you wanted to come?'

'That would be fantastic.' She kept her fingers half over her mouth. 'Thank you!'

'No problem. Give me your number and I'll text you when they're available and you can give me dates, etc.'

Cat nodded, reaching for her phone. She was really glad she hadn't set that sexy photo of Nick as her lock screen. The photo of The Rock cuddling an actual rock probably wasn't much better, but she thought she'd been fast enough that Harvey wouldn't even have noticed.

'The Rock, eh?' he said, smiling at her in that annoying way again.

'Shut up.' Cat tapped open her contacts and handed the phone to Harvey. She stared at him as he put his number in, paranoid that he'd swipe and immediately be faced with something embarrassing like porn (even though there wasn't any on her phone) (probably) or her Google history filled with searches for Sam.

'There you go,' he said, handing it back. His phone buzzed in his hand and he tapped it before saying, 'Right. We've got each other's numbers. I'll text you.'

'Thanks.'

'Bye, Harvey!' Arnold said chirpily.

'Bye,' Harvey said, looking from Cat to Arnold and back again with the same expression that Cat didn't quite understand.

'So. See you soon,' Cat said. And fled.

CHAPTER NINE

'Oh holy shit,' Cat said, as her alarm went off.

Without even moving she could feel that she'd hurt herself falling up the escalator the previous day. She winced as she reached for her phone – her neck and shoulder were stiff. Even her forearm felt a bit odd. She turned off her alarm and noticed she had a text. Scared to move, she held her phone up over her face. It was from Harvey and it said, *Good to see you again. Arnold is great.*

'Typical,' Cat muttered to herself, 'liked Arnold more than me.'

She opened Twitter and tried to shuffle her body up the bed while she confirmed that the world hadn't yet ended (but things weren't exactly looking positive). Her hips and lower back ached. And as for her inner thighs…

Once she'd managed to shuffle enough that she was propped up against her pillows, she texted Kelly: *I am broken. Come and look after me.*

Can't, Kelly replied immediately. *Got stuff to do. But I can pick you up and bring you to mine?*

Cat tapped the call button and Kelly answered straight away. 'You're on speaker,' she said. 'And Arnold's here, so—'

'Don't swear, I know.'

'Cat said "shit" yesterday,' she heard Arnold say.

'I know she did, darling,' Kelly said. 'But I think she had a good reason, don't you?'

'I do,' Cat said. 'I can barely bloody move. Sorry about the bloody.'

She heard Arnold laughing and then Kelly told him to go and get his school sweatshirt on.

'So if I pick you up after the school run,' Kelly said, 'you can come and lounge on the sofa here and I can come and have a coffee with you every now and then?'

'Don't hurt yourself,' Cat said. 'But yeah, that sounds great. You know you'll have to carry me though? I can't get out of bed.'

'And I'm pregnant, so that's not happening. Go and have a hot shower, that should help.'

'Will you give me a massage on your lunch break?'

'No.'

'Will Sean?'

Kelly laughed. 'No. Get off the phone and in the shower and I'll see you in a bit.'

'OK, thanks. Love you. Even though your son tried to murder me.'

'Saves me a job.'

'I feel like I've been beaten up,' Cat said as she lowered herself gingerly into Kelly's car. 'Every single bit of me hurts.'

'I still laugh every time I picture it,' Kelly said, pulling out of the space in front of Cat's flat.

'Oh, I'm sure it looked hilarious. But I felt like I was going to be ripped in half. Forced splits? On an escalator?'

Kelly let out a bark of laughter.

'How are you laughing? I left your child at the bottom! On his own! Anything could have happened to him!'

'In John Lewis?!'

'Bad things happen in John Lewis, Kelly. I got stuck in a knee-high boot once. Took two members of staff to free me.'

Kelly snorted again. 'That was Selfridges. I was with you.'

'Oh yeah.'

'I still think you should've bought them.'

It was Cat's turn to snort. 'They were super hot. But I had the imprint of the zip on my calf for weeks.'

Cat turned to look out of the window as Kelly pulled out onto the main road.

'So tell me about Harvey,' Kelly said and Cat felt something flutter in her belly. That was weird.

'Nothing to tell really,' Cat said. 'He was there. We had cake. He was really good with Arnold.'

'Arnold's in love with him. Has not stopped talking about him. He was so funny and nice and he didn't tell Arnold he smells…'

'Amateur.'

'He said he's going to get tickets for the panto?'

'So he said, yeah.'

'And you exchanged numbers? Arnold was very impressed that he rang himself from your phone.'

'Oh Arnold. Get it together. Oldest trick in the book.'

'But yeah. He works at a theatre? In lighting?'

'Did Arnold remember that?'

'Nah, I googled him.'

'Ugh. There's no mystery any more.'

'Like you haven't googled him – all of them – every day since we saw Sam.'

'I have not!' Except she had. 'But I've stalked them all on Facebook.'

'I bet you can add him now. After yesterday.'

Cat had actually wondered the same thing. She'd sat in bed that morning, propped up on all her pillows because her neck felt like she had whiplash, and hovered her finger over the 'add friend' button. But how could she be Harvey's friend and not Sam's? Sam would see they were friends and would definitely find that weird. And if Jan saw, then she'd add her too. And then Cat would have to add Sam and how would that even work? She didn't have any of her exes on Facebook as was right and good.

And if she searched them all by name every time she had more than two glasses of wine, no one needed to know.

Cat lay on Kelly's sofa, a cushion behind her neck, another under the small of her back, a cup of tea and a packet of biscuits on the table next to her and *The Greatest Showman* on the TV. Even her phone was charging.

'How are you such a grown-up?' she asked Kelly, trying to tip her head back to look at her upside down, but wincing with pain instead. 'And why does every bit of me hurt.'

'I think it's cos you brace yourself against falling. It happened to me when I fell down the stairs carrying Arnold, remember?'

Cat had seen it happen and been impressed at how her friend had curled herself around the baby with no regard for herself. Luckily she'd only scraped her elbow and bruised her little toe, but the following day she'd barely been able to move.

'And how are you still not a grown-up?' Kelly added, but she leaned down and kissed Cat on the forehead. 'Text me if you need me. Don't shout, cos I won't hear you. And also please don't text cos I've got work to do.'

Cat watched the film over the top of her phone while she caught up on all of the internet. She spent the entire Bearded Lady song staring at Harvey's Facebook and wondering about adding him. She could just add him, surely. That would be a normal thing to do. They'd bumped into each other twice now, they got on well – they'd always got on well. If he wasn't Sam's brother she'd have done it already. But. He *was* Sam's brother.

Maybe she should add Sam? She tapped over to Sam's profile and the top post was the announcement of another stand-up show at a different venue. A smaller one. One that Cat had actually performed at too. It was the upstairs of a pub and known as a place where comedians workshopped or tried out new material.

Sometimes huge names would perform there, unannounced. She and Sam had seen Gemma Jewell there once and she'd blown them both away. Just thinking about standing on that stage made Cat's fingertips tingle.

'Now this is sponcon,' Kelly said when they broke for lunch, sliding a white bowl in front of Cat. It was filled with greens along with chunks of orange and avocado and something purple Cat didn't recognise.

Although it wasn't much of a break because Kelly had made the lunch and then photographed it on the floor with her lightbox. Cat had been amazed the first time she'd seen Kelly do it; she'd previously assumed her friend was just better at taking and filtering phone photos than she was, but no, it was a whole thing.

'I thought you were doing beans on toast,' Cat said, poking at the salad with her fork.

Kelly rolled her eyes. 'Just eat it. It's good for you.'

'Too healthy,' Cat said, avoiding the purple stuff and popping a chunk of orange into her mouth. 'Body might go into shock.' She swallowed the orange and speared some avocado. 'This is really good, Kel!'

'Thanks.' Kelly was poking at hers with her fork, but Cat hadn't seen her eat any yet.

'You feeling sick?'

Kelly shook her head. 'Not sick. I just don't fancy it.'

'What do you fancy then?'

Kelly shook her head again. 'I don't even want to say. I'm too embarrassed.'

'Is it Alan Titchmarsh?'

Kelly snorted. 'He's got some lovely jumpers. Wait. I'll show you.'

'You've nicked one of his jumpers? Get it, girl.'

Kelly rolled her eyes again and climbed down off the stool, crossing the room and opening the door to her enormous hidden larder. Cat had been over to the house dozens of times before she even knew it was there – she'd thought the doors along the back of the room were ordinary cupboards. And then one day Kelly had opened one and disappeared. If it had been Cat's house, she'd have turned it into a karaoke room or put in a flotation tank – something unexpected anyway – but, because it was Kelly, it was actually simply lined with shelves stacked with 'store-cupboard staples' and apparently ever-replenishing boxes of basics like loo roll and teabags. Although there was a corner drawer of biscuits and chocolate that Cat and Arnold had been known to raid whenever Cat babysat.

When Kelly reappeared she looked shifty, her cheeks pink. She had a bright yellow can in each hand and as she approached Cat, she held them out to her.

'Macaroni cheese,' Cat said, bemused.

'Not just macaroni cheese,' Kelly said, already reaching for a tin opener. 'Really shit stuff. The cheapest, most disgusting, kind. Full of colourings and E-numbers and nothing found in nature.'

'So?' Cat said.

She actually quite fancied a bowl herself, but she had to admit she was enjoying the fancy salad more than she'd thought she would. She'd even eaten some greenery.

'So I'm meant to be eating healthily for the baby,' Kelly said, almost writhing with embarrassment as she poured the contents of the can into a bowl and pushed it into the microwave. 'The midwife told me that before I eat anything, I should ask myself if it's the best thing for the baby, no, the best bite. Three Bs: Best Bite for Baby.'

'That's BBfB,' Cat said through a mouthful of lettuce. 'Best bite baby seems like terrible advice to me.'

'I've tried,' Kelly said, ignoring her. 'But every time I make something healthy it makes me gag. The only stuff I want to eat is garbage.'

'So.' Cat shrugged. 'Shouldn't you just eat what you want? Or what you *can*? It's not actually going to affect the baby, is it?'

'But what if it does?' Kelly said. 'What if it comes out all pasty and glowing like those fish in *The Simpsons*.'

'From macaroni cheese?'

'From shit, canned macaroni cheese, heated in the microwave.'

Right on cue, the timer pinged and Kelly sighed as she removed the dish and sat back down.

'A couple of weeks ago,' she said, lowering her face to sniff the steam rising from the plate, 'I woke up in the night with cramp in my leg. And I had a banana on the bedside table because they're full of potassium and that's good for cramp.'

'I'm glad you told me that. Cos if I'd seen a banana on your bedside table it would have made me look at Sean in an entirely different light.'

'I peeled it,' Kelly said. 'But I couldn't even get it near my mouth—'

'We've all been there.'

'So I came downstairs and had macaroni cheese. Cold. From the can. I didn't even properly take the lid off, just folded it back.'

'You're a monster,' Cat said. 'I don't think we can be friends. Can I tell you something mad?'

'Oh god,' Kelly said.

'I told Harvey I was doing stand-up again. Or planning to. I can't remember.'

'Why did you do that?'

Cat sighed. 'I think because I didn't have anything good to tell him, you know? Like I didn't want him to go to one of the big family meals and say he'd seen me and when they asked how I was he'd have to say "oh, you know, the same, living in a shithole, working in a shithole, still not even doing stand-up".'

'Your hair's better though,' Kelly said. She'd already eaten about half of the bowl, sighing with happiness the entire time. 'And you mean Sam. You don't want Sam to think you're still stuck in the same job you were back then.'

'Maybe,' Cat said, even though she knew Kelly was right. 'Can I ask you something?'

'You know you can.'

'Why did I stop doing stand-up? In your opinion?'

Kelly put her fork down and stared across the table at Cat. 'And I can answer this, right? Without you losing your shit?'

'Of course!'

'You say that, but we had this conversation once before. Or at least I tried to. And you did a runner.'

'I didn't,' Cat said. 'You threw me out.'

Kelly shook her head. 'I haven't got the strength for this argument again.'

'OK,' Cat said. 'But I'm going nowhere this time. My thighs aren't up to it.'

'OK,' Kelly said. And then, gently, 'I think because you got scared.'

She slumped off the stool again and opened the metal armadillo bread bin before cutting herself a thick slice and slathering it with butter.

'You've got more butter than bread there,' Cat said.

'I would actually eat the butter on its own if it was socially acceptable.'

'Knock yourself out,' Cat said. 'I would pay to see that.'

Kelly pulled a face. 'Stop avoiding the conversation.'

'Me? I'm just sitting here.'

'I think you got scared and it was easier to stop doing it than to, you know, be scared.'

Cat stared at her as she took an enormous bite of the bread and then dipped the crust into the Day-Glo yellow of the macaroni cheese.

'I wasn't scared. I was good at it.'

'That,' Kelly said, her mouth full of bread, 'is what scared you.'

'That doesn't make sense.' She cut herself a slice of bread and covered it in only slightly less butter than Kelly's. 'I was only OK. And I didn't want to—'

'You were good,' Kelly said. 'Better than Sam.'

'I was not.'

'You were. That show you did in Ealing? You killed it. And Sam was good, but not as good as you. And he knew it too. He told me.'

'He told you I was better than him?'

Kelly nodded.

Cat couldn't believe it.

'What did he say exactly?'

'God, I don't know. It was five years ago! But I remember cos when I was watching him I was wondering how he'd feel about you being better. You know, it could go either way, right? Some men would lose their shit. And others – like Sean – would love it. He'd support me if I walked into his office today and swiped his job from under him. I could be his boss and he'd just be all "proud of you, babe".'

Cat smiled. She was right. 'You'd have to find out exactly what he does first.'

Kelly laughed. 'It doesn't matter. As long as he's happy. And I'm not going to do it, obviously. But, like, Dark Dave would've—'

'Ugh,' Cat said. She'd hated Dark Dave.

'I know. I know we said we'd never speak of him again, but he's the perfect example for this!'

'God. Go on then.'

'Dark Dave would've hated it. He'd have belittled me. Probably in front of everyone else. He'd have told me that everyone was laughing out of embarrassment. I mean, if it was something he did too – like stand-up – I wouldn't even have got that far; he'd have destroyed my confidence long before I saw a stage. He'd have been threatened. Sam wasn't like that. I don't think he was quite as laid-back as Sean either; I felt like he was a bit jealous? Maybe? But he told me you were great and that he was proud of you and I hugged him.'

Cat remembered the hug. She'd seen it as she was coming down the few steps from the stage. She remembered because she'd thought Sam was leaving, that he'd watched her set and he was going home. Because he was pissed off. She'd spent the rest of the evening – after they'd both performed – asking him if he was OK. She remembered that too because when they were in bed at home – Sam's flat – later, after they'd had sex (she was sure they'd had sex, they generally did when they stayed at Sam's), she'd been almost asleep with her face pressed into the curve of his neck, one arm across his chest, her thigh hooked over his, when she'd said, 'You're not going to leave me, are you?'

And Sam had pretended to be asleep.

CHAPTER TEN

Cat was dozing, propped up against her pillows, mindlessly playing the dots game, when her phone rang and made her jump. Harvey. It was Harvey. Why was he calling instead of texting? Who the hell actually *called* people on their phones any more? She should just let it go to voicemail and then never listen to it (who listened to voicemails any more?). Instead she answered and said, 'Who even calls people any more?'

Harvey's low laugh rumbled through her ear and headed south. 'Sorry, is it too late?'

'About ten years too late,' Cat said, clicking her bedside lamp back on. 'Everyone just texts now. Did you not get the memo?'

'Must've missed it,' he said. 'But, like, you're not in bed or anything, are you?'

'No,' Cat lied. 'I've just been…' she glanced around the room, trying to come up with an idea for something interesting she could reasonably have been doing '…watching Netflix,' she said instead.

'Me too,' he said, and she could hear the smile in his voice. The voice that was even deeper and sexier on a mobile; it was awful. 'I'm on a break. And I had an idea.'

'Yeah?'

'I don't know if you'd be interested, but when you come to the panto, you could come early and I can give you a tour of the theatre. It's not huge, but it's pretty cool and I thought Arnold might like it?'

'He'd love that,' Cat said. 'He's got a massive crush on you. Hasn't shut up about you since that day in John Lewis.'

Harvey laughed. 'He's a really cute kid.'

'He is. He's great.' She reached for her glass of water on the bedside table. 'I— shit!' She knocked it off, water pouring down the front and soaking the pile of magazines on the floor next to the bed.

'You OK?' Harvey asked.

'Yeah.' Cat leaned over and peered at the mess. 'Sorry. Just knocked a glass of water over.'

'Do you need to go and sort it out?'

'Nah. Thanks. This flat's a tip anyway. I can call it cleaning.'

'Where are you living now?' Harvey asked.

'Queen's Park. Well, Kilburn. Border of. No one can quite decide. What about you? You've got a new place, right?'

Shit.

There was a short silence on the other end of the line and then Harvey said, 'Did I mention that when I saw you?'

'Um,' Cat said. 'OK. Don't judge me. I saw it on Facebook.'

He laughed. 'Are you stalking me?'

'Yes,' Cat said. 'Look out of the window. I'm crouched between the bins. Listen, everyone looks people up on Facebook and if they say they don't they're lying.'

'I don't.'

'You're lying.'

'I'm not. I really don't. I barely use it.'

'You didn't look me up? After seeing me at Sam's show?' She actually felt a little disappointed.

'I didn't. But only cos I don't really use it. If I was a professional online stalker like apparently everyone else, I totally would've done.'

'Right,' Cat said. 'Helpful.'

'So what do you think?' Harvey asked.

'About Facebook?'

'About the tour. And the panto.'

'Sounds great. When's good for you?'

'How's the boyfriend?' Nick asked, coming up behind Cat at work the following morning.

She really needed to turn her desk round. Although then she'd just be surprised from the other side.

'Oh, he's not,' Cat said. 'I misunderstood the question. Last time.'

'Yeah?' Nick said. 'You misunderstood "Is that your boyfriend"?'

'Let it go,' Cat said.

Nick grinned. 'Is Colin in?'

'He's not actually. He should be back fairly soon. If you wanted to wait in his office?'

Nick sat on the chair on the opposite side of Cat's desk. 'I'll sit here, I think. If that's OK with you?'

He was already swivelling the chair from side to side, one foot up on the opposite knee. Cat shook her head. 'That's fine, yeah. Can I get you a drink?'

'No, I'm good, thanks.' He held up a Starbucks cup. 'Busy?'

'Yes, actually,' she said, double-checking that her screen wasn't still showing Facebook. She'd been sitting and staring into space for so long that she'd totally missed Nick coming in. 'Thinking time is important to the creative process.'

Nick did the grinning with his tongue in his cheek thing that went straight to Cat's groin. She'd always thought 'tongue-in-cheek' was just an expression until she met Nick. She remembered Kelly telling her to sleep with him. She'd remembered it a few times in the week or so since their conversation. But it wasn't going to happen.

'So what have you come up with?' Nick asked. 'Creative accounting-wise.'

'Hmm?' She glanced around her desk for a glass of water or just anything to distract herself with, occupy her hands, but there was nothing. She tapped at her keyboard briefly.

'Your creative daydreaming session,' Nick said. 'Did you come up with anything?'

She pictured Nick in the conference room, undoing his shirt and crawling across the table. Crawling? What the fuck?

'Just something I'm considering for the invoicing,' she said instead, and mentally kicked herself. *Be more boring, Cat.*

Nick grinned at her. 'I look forward to hearing about it.'

'Well,' Cat said. 'You'll be gone. So.'

Nick nodded, still smiling at her. 'I learned something about you the other day.' He reached across her desk and picked something up between his thumb and forefinger.

Cat couldn't see what it was. She hoped it wasn't something gross like a bit of fingernail she'd chewed and flicked.

'Yeah?'

'You used to do stand-up?'

'Oh my god! How did you find out about that?!'

'Edinburgh Festival website. My sister lives up there and she said I should come up for it next year – she's not happy about me moving to New York, so she's trying to get me to commit to future plans – so I was just idly googling and… there you were.'

'God,' Cat said, wondering if any of that was true or if he'd just been googling her. The thought made her heart race. 'That feels like a long time ago.'

Just the thought of it was making the hairs on the back of her neck stand up. It had been the best thing she'd ever done. The best audience. One of those nights – well, it wasn't a night, it was the middle of the afternoon – that she'd just nailed it. She thought about it sometimes when she couldn't get to sleep, ran

over her entire set in her head. Some bits still made her laugh.
She could smell the room – dust and paper and beer – and see
some of the faces in the audience. It had been her happy place.

'I bet you were good,' Nick said.

Cat laughed. 'Based on what?'

Nick did that smile again and leaned forward, his elbows on
her desk. 'Just a feeling. Were you?'

'What?'

'Good?'

Cat closed her eyes for a second, remembered her conversation
with Kelly (she'd been *better than Sam*), opened them, and said,
'Actually yeah, I was.'

'So why'd you stop?'

Cat shrugged. 'Just, you know, life.'

Nick nodded. 'Seems like a shame. If you loved it.'

'Yeah,' Cat said.

The main doors opened and Colin burst in, shaking rain off
his coat and muttering to no one in particular about the weather,
before saying, 'Nick? You ready?', as if Nick hadn't been the one
waiting for him.

'Right,' Nick said to Cat, pushing himself to standing, as Colin
disappeared inside his office. 'I'll be off then.' He held his hand
out, his palm flat. There was a penny there, dull and brown. 'This
was on your desk. Sorry, I like to fiddle when I chat.'

Cat couldn't resist raising one eyebrow, but she took the penny,
her fingers brushing Nick's. 'Thanks.'

Nick glanced over his shoulder at Colin's office. 'We should
get a coffee one day, actually. Somewhere that's not here.'

Cat's stomach fluttered and she took a breath, squeezing the
penny in her fist. It had been on her desk because she'd found
it on the way to work one day, weeks ago. *See a penny, pick it
up, all day long you'll have good luck.* She thought about how
Nick had clearly been googling her. She thought about Sam

and Harvey and Kelly and how long it had been since she'd even been kissed.

'Actually,' she said, 'I've got these theatre tickets. It's a new play in a really small venue, but it's meant to be good. Maybe we—'

Nick's brow was furrowed and Cat already felt like she may have made a terrible mistake. He stepped a little closer and dipped his head.

'I, ah, when I said about coffee, I meant to talk about work. I didn't mean… I'm sorry if I gave the impression—'

'Oh my god,' Cat said, her face burning. 'No. You didn't. It was me, I—'

'I'm gay,' Nick said, his voice low. 'I'm sorry; I thought you knew that. I mean, if I wasn't then—'

Cat shook her head and then couldn't seem to stop shaking it. She must've looked like a Golden Retriever with water on the ear.

'It's fine,' she said. 'Sorry. I hope that wasn't… I mean…'

'No,' Nick said. 'You're fine. I'm sorry if I made you uncomfortable, or—'

'God,' Cat said. 'No. I need to…' She glanced around wildly. There was nothing she needed to do. 'Loo. I need the loo. I'll see you… another… yeah.'

'Wow,' Kelly said when Cat phoned her from the toilet stall. After she'd banged her head against the door approximately forty-six times.

'I know.'

'I mean… wow.'

'I know!' Cat said. 'Shut up.'

'You didn't know he was gay?'

'Obviously!'

'The work thing's interesting though.'

Cat usually wouldn't slump in a work loo, but she was slumped now, her head against the side of the stall. She'd have to disinfect her entire body when she got home.

'Oh, it won't be. He might want me to move to the Soho Square office, since he's not going to be there.' She banged her head on the side. It hurt much more than her forehead; she probably wouldn't do that again. 'Why am I such an idiot?'

'You're not an idiot,' Kelly said.

Cat snorted.

'I mean, obviously you are. But I'm still proud of you! You took a chance! You seized the day. It's not your fault the day turned out to be gay.'

'You're not funny.'

'I'm a bit funny.'

Cat stood up and the loo flushed automatically behind her, even though she hadn't used it. She let herself out and stared at herself in the long mirror that ran along the wall. She had a red mark on her forehead.

'Want to talk more about Nick?' Kelly asked.

'God. No. I want to go and get drunk. But instead I guess I'll make a start on some VAT Returns.'

'Yeah. Treat yourself.'

Cat pulled a face in the mirror.

'The thing is,' Kelly said, 'It's not the most embarrassing thing you've ever done and you'll probably do something even more embarrassing in the future.'

'Yeah?' Cat said. 'And? What?'

'Oh, that's it. I'm just saying.' She cackled.

'I hate you,' Cat said.

Cat got home to find Georgie and her boyfriend had a bunch of friends round and they were all loudly playing Cards Against

Humanity in the living room. On the way home, she'd been thinking about making herself spaghetti bolognaise and garlic bread and eating it in front of the TV, but she couldn't face it any more.

She made a peanut butter sandwich and a cup of tea and took them to her room. When she'd first moved in, Georgie – who'd had a different boyfriend – had tried to include her, but after a few awkward evenings they realised they had nothing in common and would never actually be friends. Cat knew that Georgie thought she was boring, but after a long day at work, she wanted to be able to relax at home – get into her pyjamas and curl up in front of the TV with a cup of tea and a bag of Hula Hoops; she didn't want to be expected to entertain.

Sitting on her bed, she was alternating scrolling through Instagram on her phone and trying to pick something to watch on Netflix on her laptop, when she got a text from her dad.

All it said was *I'm heading over your way soon. You free to meet up? Dad* but it made Cat's stomach sink. She didn't want to see him. Did she? She wasn't actually sure.

No, that wasn't strictly true. She was sure she didn't want to see him. But knowing that to be the case made her feel like shit.

CHAPTER ELEVEN

Harvey met them at the stage door, which was already pretty exciting for both Cat and Arnold. It had been sleeting all morning and once inside the theatre, Cat unwound Arnold's scarf and then her own, pulling their hats off their heads and watching as Arnold's hair stuck straight up with static before settling down again. Cat smoothed it with her hand then leaned down to sniff it.

'Pipe smoke,' she said. 'And good cheese. Did you spend last night in a gentleman's club by any chance?'

Arnold laughed. 'No! I just went to bed.'

'Interesting,' Cat said. 'I don't suppose you can prove it?'

Arnold giggled and Cat looked up to find Harvey watching them both with that odd, slightly distant expression on his face.

'It's a bit,' Cat said. 'We've always done it.'

'Cute,' Harvey said.

They followed him up the stairs, past the dressing rooms from where different music was pouring. He knocked on one door and introduced them both, but mostly Arnold, to the CBeebies presenter who played Buttons. Arnold's mouth hung open and he curled into Cat's side, looking up from under his fringe, shyly.

The presenter had signed a programme for Arnold and then they'd left, Harvey pulling the door closed behind him.

'How long have you worked here?' Cat asked him as they walked down another corridor strewn with cables, the walls covered with old show posters, the curling edges stuck down with tape.

'Here?' Harvey said, glancing back over his shoulder.

Cat noticed the muscles moving under his white T-shirt and looked down at the ground instead; she really didn't want to trip over any of the health and safety hazards that seemed to be round every corner.

'I've only been here just under six months,' Harvey continued. 'I worked in the Richmond Theatre before. You've been there, right?'

Cat nodded. She and Sam had gone with his parents after dinner by the side of the river. It had been one of Cat's all-time favourite nights.

'So I started there as a trainee lighting tech,' Harvey said. 'And then I saw this job advertised and... I was happy there, but it was always my dream to work in the West End.'

'I never knew that,' Cat said. Although there wasn't really any reason why she would have done. While she and Sam were together, she and Harvey had always got on well, but they never exactly had deep and meaningful conversations. Except that one night in the garden that Cat wasn't going to think about right now.

They followed Harvey up a couple of flights of narrow stairs and onto a catwalk above the small auditorium.

'Woah!' Arnold said, his eyes wide. He backed up towards the wall, but Harvey said, 'Do you want to go out there?'

The lights were arranged above a mesh net over the auditorium.

'You can go out on it?' Cat asked. 'Seriously?'

'We have to,' Harvey said. 'To work the lights.'

He explained to them how they could move the lighting around depending on the requirements of different shows, and as he talked, he stepped out onto the net. Cat gasped as it dipped under his weight, but watched in awe as he ducked under lights, moving them along the metal construction, the muscles shifting in his back.

'Want to come out here?' he asked Arnold, holding out his hand.

Arnold shook his head.

'You sure?' Cat asked him.

'You go first,' Arnold told her.

Shit. She really didn't want to.

'I don't think you can have two grown-ups out there at the same time,' she told Arnold.

'You can.' Harvey shrugged. 'I think the limit's meant to be four, but we've had six out before now. Two is fine.' He held his hand out to Cat. 'You up for it?'

Cat glanced down at Arnold and the expression on his face confirmed that he actually did want to do it; he just didn't quite trust Harvey enough yet. But he trusted Cat. Damn.

Stepping up to the edge of the metal frame, she reached out for Harvey with one hand, while keeping her other on the frame. Harvey's warm hand engulfed hers and for a second she had a vision of herself plummeting through the mesh, with Harvey's hold on her hand the only thing preventing her from certain death. She felt Harvey squeeze her fingers and he said, 'You want to come out further? Let go of the…'

Cat peeled her other hand away and gasped as she felt the net dip again. She knew she was holding Harvey's hand extremely tight, but there was no way she was going to let go.

She turned to look at Arnold, plastering a bright smile on her face. 'Want to come out here? It's really cool.'

Arnold took a tentative step towards Cat. She reached for his hand and steered him out onto the mesh.

'You can jump,' Harvey said, bending his knees.

'Don't you dare,' Cat said through gritted teeth.

Harvey laughed and bumped her with his shoulder. And they were still holding hands. She should probably let go. She didn't want to. Harvey showed Arnold some lighting effects and Cat was still holding his hand. He told Arnold how the lights could be detached completely and moved to different parts of the theatre and Cat was still holding his hand. He took a photo of Arnold on his phone and Cat was still holding his hand. When they finally stepped off the mesh and back onto solid ground, Cat's knees felt wobbly. Harvey squeezed her fingers and then let go.

'Want to go on the stage?' Harvey asked Arnold.

Arnold nodded, his eyes bright with anticipation.

They followed Harvey back down the stairs, him describing everything they were seeing and telling them little anecdotes the entire way and then they were in the auditorium and following him out into the middle of the stage. Cat looked out at the seats stretching up towards the roof.

'You see the mesh?' Harvey asked Arnold, pointing. 'We were just standing up there.'

'I can see my hat,' Arnold said.

'What?' Cat hadn't even noticed he'd taken it off. But there it was, bright yellow against the red mesh.

Harvey laughed and ruffled Arnold's hair. 'You OK to stay here while I go and get it?'

Arnold nodded.

Harvey smiled at Cat, said, 'Two minutes,' and disappeared through a door at the side of the stage.

'There's no one here!' Arnold said and Cat laughed.

'Did you think you were coming out to be in the show?' Cat asked him.

When Arnold nodded, Cat pulled him closer and gave him a quick squeeze. 'Wow, you're brave,' she told him. 'I feel a bit nervous even though it's empty.' She took a deep breath, turning slowly to take everything in.

'Did you know I used to go onstage?' she asked Arnold.

'On *X Factor*?' Arnold asked.

Cat laughed. 'No, I was a comedian. I told jokes.'

'I know a joke!' Arnold said, his eyes shining.

'Go on…'

'Why did the chicken cross the road?'

'I don't know. Why did the chicken cross the road?'

'Cos it wanted to see the other chicken that got run over.'

'Dark,' Cat said. 'I like it.'

Arnold stretched his arms out and turned in a slow circle, like Cat had just done. 'Did you do jokes here?'

'No,' Cat said. 'Never anywhere as big as this.'

She stared out at the stalls. No, she'd never played a theatre. Not even close. But it still felt familiar. Just being on a stage. The smell of the auditorium. The idea of looking out and seeing so many faces looking back at you. Expecting you to be funny.

She hadn't realised how much she missed it.

CHAPTER TWELVE

Cat was thinking she should probably get out of bed and cross the room and turn off the birdsong alarm on her phone, which she'd left on the window ledge to prevent her ignoring her alarm, when there was a knock at the door.

'I'm awake!' she croaked.

The door opened and Kelly crept in, holding a mug of tea.

After bringing Arnold back the previous day, Cat had ended up staying for dinner and then the night. It was always hard to leave Kelly's house – it was so warm and cosy and fun and no one ever stole her beers and cracked any necks or had really loud sex in the living room.

'I'm up,' Cat repeated, shuffling up the bed to lean back against the pillows. 'You're too nice.'

Kelly put the tea down on the bedside table and sat down heavily at the bottom of the bed. 'I've been up since four, puking.'

Cat's eyes hadn't focused properly and the room was mostly still dark, but she blinked and then squinted and she could see that Kelly did look pale. And tired.

'Get in with me,' Cat said, folding back the other side of the duvet.

'You'll be late.' Kelly shook her head.

'I don't care. You're more important. Come on.'

Kelly clambered into bed next to Cat and dropped her head down on her shoulder.

'I feel like shit.'

Cat stroked her hair. 'I'm not surprised.'

'I'm so sick of feeling sick all the time. I wasn't like this with Arnold.'

'You weren't sick at all with Arnold, were you?'

'Only once. When we were watching *Eternal Sunshine of the Spotless Mind*. I threw up in—'

'A Quality Street tin. Yeah, it's all coming back to me now.'

'I can't decide if it's better being sick or just feeling sick all the time.'

'Worst "Would You Rather?" ever,' Cat said.

'Would you rather get back with Sam or go out with Harvey?' Kelly said.

Cat jerked her head back so fast, she banged it against the headboard.

'Sorry,' Kelly said. 'I was thinking about it when I was lying on the bathroom floor.'

'God,' Cat said. 'I don't... God. There's nothing going on with Harvey.'

'But there could be.'

'No,' Cat said. 'No way. He's Sam's brother. He's off limits.'

'Bollocks.'

'He is. There's just no way.'

'Does he know that?'

'He doesn't need to. He's not interested in me.'

'Are you sure? He was flirty at the show, you said.'

'He's always flirty, it doesn't mean anything.'

'And then he invited you to the theatre where you had, according to Arnold, the best day ever.'

'That was because of Arnold. He invited me cos of Arnold.'

'How do you know?'

'Because he's nice. He's nice and good with kids and charming and funny and hot.'

'Wow, you're really not interested,' Kelly said. 'I stand corrected.'

'Shut up,' Cat said and slurped her tea because she knew it would annoy her friend.

'You're allowed to just have fun,' Kelly said. 'It doesn't need to be a big relationship thing.'

'I mean, it literally couldn't be a big relationship thing,' Cat said. 'That's not even—'

'So just a shag then. I bet he's good.'

'I haven't thought about it,' Cat lied. She absolutely had not fallen asleep last night thinking of shagging Harvey on that stupid terrifying net. Or in the dressing room, in front of one of the mirrors surrounded by lights. Or actually on the stage in front of a full theatre (that one had been a bit weird).

'I know you're lying,' Kelly said. 'You forget that I know you better than you know—' The colour suddenly drained out of her face and she lurched up and over the side of the bed to throw up on the floor.

'Yourself,' she said, weakly, a few seconds later.

'I'm sorry, I can't come in today,' Cat said. She was lying on her back on the bed, her head dangling over the side to make her voice sound suitably strained. 'Yeah, I think it was something I ate.'

Colin sounded distracted and pissed off, but Cat didn't even feel guilty. Her work was up to date; they could definitely manage without her for a day and Kelly was more important. After Kelly had been sick, Cat had cleaned it up (gagging and with her eyes mostly closed) and then put Kelly to bed. Then she'd got Arnold up and made him breakfast – a marmalade sandwich so he could pretend to be Paddington – and then she'd phoned Colin.

'Do you know the way to school?' she asked Arnold now. 'We'll have to walk.'

'Why do we?'

'Because your mum's not feeling very well and I can't drive her car. Or anyone's car.'

'Why can't Daddy drive me?'

'Because he's away with work. Which is why I'm here. Now can you go and wipe your face, you've given yourself a Glasgow smile with marmalade.'

'What's a Glasgow smile?'

'Never mind that. Have you got a bag or something?'

'I think Mummy leaves it by the door.'

While Arnold went to wash his face, Cat looked for the bag. He was right – next to the door was a small pile of oblong wooden boxes that Cat had noticed and admired in passing, but never realised had any practical purpose. One was yellow with the Coca-Cola logo in red and held Arnold's shoes. Another – brown and printed with *Covent Garden Flower Market* – contained a flat blue bag which, when Cat looked, had a reading book and some paperwork inside. Kelly was so bloody organised, it was ridiculous.

'Right,' Cat said to Arnold, as he stepped out of the downstairs loo. 'Get your shoes and coat on and we'll get going.'

Outside, it was bright and cold – Cat's favourite weather.

'It's not far, is it?' Cat said. She'd been in the car plenty of times, but found it hard to translate driving distance to walking distance.

She took Arnold's hand as they stepped out onto the street. Cat looked around, hoping she'd see some other parents heading the same way that she could just follow, but no such luck. They crossed the main road and Cat felt fairly confident Kelly usually turned left, so that's what they did.

'Why is Mummy sick?' Arnold asked, as they passed a newsagent's and Cat made a mental note to stop off there on the way back and get a magazine and some chocolate for Kelly.

And maybe ginger ale? That was meant to be good for morning sickness, she was sure.

'Because of the baby in her tummy,' Cat said. There was still no sign of any other kids, but she decided to plough on.

'Why does it make her sick?' Arnold asked.

Cat stopped walking and looked down at him. 'You know what? I don't know. It's probably hormones. It's usually hormones.'

'What's hormones?'

Cat started walking again. 'I don't think I know that either. I'll google it and tell you when you get home. Or you could ask your teacher, I'd bet they'd like that.'

They crossed another road – Cat was almost certain it was the right way.

'I don't want a baby brother,' Arnold said.

When Cat looked down at him, he looked furious, his forehead furrowed, cheeks pink, lower lip pouched out.

'Well, first of all,' Cat said, 'that's just tough. The baby's coming whether you like it or not. But, you know what? You might love it so much you can't believe it.'

'I don't love it,' Arnold said.

'I know you don't love it now. But I bet you will when you meet it. And it will annoy you and sometimes you'll wish you were an only child, but then other times you'll be so happy to have them.'

'What's yours called?' Arnold asked. And then skipped a little on the spot and shouted, 'JACOB!'

'Who on earth is Jacob?' Cat asked.

'My friend! Over there! He's got a Nintendo Switch in his bedroom.'

'Wow. Lucky Jacob. At least that means we're definitely going the right way.'

Jacob was waving from the other side of the road and Arnold was almost vibrating with excitement.

'Is it a boy or a girl?' Arnold asked.

'Jacob? You'd know better than me, but I was assuming boy.'

'No! Your sister.' He looked up at her as if he couldn't believe how thick she was being.

'I haven't got a sister,' Cat said.

She could see more children in the distance now. They seemed to be appearing out of every side road to form a river of children pouring towards the school. Like Avengers Assembling. Or maybe zombies.

'What's your brother called?'

'I haven't got a brother either.'

'What have you got then?' Arnold said.

'Just me.'

'And your mummy.'

'Nope, no mummy either. Just me and my dad.' Who she still hadn't called. Even though he'd texted again, more than once.

'My dad's in Birmingham,' Arnold said.

'I know. I told *you* that.'

At the school gates, Cat kissed Arnold on the crown of his head and said, 'Marmalade, coffee and bear breath,' which caused him to breathe in her face and reminded her that she'd forgotten to get him to clean his teeth, which was one of the things Kelly had said they had to do before leaving for school. Oh well.

Of course 'Did you clean his teeth?' was the first thing Kelly asked when she woke up. It was coming up to eleven and Cat had been lying on the sofa half-watching *This Morning* while scrolling through the internet on her phone.

'Course,' she said. 'And I spat on a tissue and cleaned his face. No. I forgot. But it'll be fine. How are you feeling?'

'Rough. But I need to eat something.' She opened the door to the secret larder. 'Have you eaten?' Her voice echoed from the small room.

'I had some toast, yeah.'

'Do you want some custard?'

'Custard?' Cat rolled off the sofa and followed Kelly into the larder. 'Just custard?'

'Yeah. I keep thinking about it.'

'Are you only craving yellow things? First the macaroni cheese, and the banana, now custard?'

'I had a mustard sandwich yesterday. It burned my tongue, but it was so good.'

'Weird.'

'Do you want some?'

'Yeah, go on then. I'll do it.'

Kelly sat on the sofa while Cat heated up a carton of custard and then they both sat at the kitchen island to eat it.

'I can't remember the last time I had custard,' Cat said. And then as she lifted the spoon to her mouth she realised why. She was back in the kitchen at her nan's. Ken Bruce's voice was coming out of the radio on the window ledge. The back door was open, wind rippling the multicoloured plastic fly curtain. Someone was standing in the archway between the kitchen and dining room. She couldn't remember who it was, but she knew she didn't want to talk to them.

'My nan used to make egg mashed up in a cup,' she told Kelly, pushing the bowl of custard away. 'That's mostly yellow. You should try that.'

'What is it?' Kelly had almost finished her bowl of custard already.

'Well, I feel like the clue is in the name,' Cat said. 'But basically it's a soft boiled egg. Mashed up. In a cup. With loads of butter and salt and pepper.'

Kelly nodded. 'That sounds amazing. Do you know how to make it?'

'It's an egg in a cup, Kel, I'm not completely incapable! I made this lovely custard, didn't I?'

'You heated it in the microwave, yeah.'

'Well, boiling an egg is basically the same. I can never really get the yolk to be soft, to be honest, but I'll give it a go.'

'Are you not going to eat that?'

Cat pushed her custard over for Kelly.

'I've been invited to the launch of some new bar off Carnaby Street. Do you want to go? It sounds nuts. It's a forest. With tents and firepits.'

'Sounds like a health and safety nightmare.'

'Right? But there's free food and drink and it might be fun. You could ask Harvey if he wanted to go…' She stared down into her custard.

'Why would I do that?'

Kelly rolled her eyes. 'Why not? You like him. He likes you – don't argue! You might, you know, have fun.'

'Ugh,' Cat said. 'I hate fun.'

'I know, darling. But you should try to have some anyway.'

CHAPTER THIRTEEN

Cat had spent the best part of a week telling herself there was no way she was going to invite Harvey to the launch, and then she'd invited him. As she'd known she would from the moment Kelly had mentioned it. It was near to the theatre, Cat had told him, which was why she'd thought of asking him. Not that he'd questioned it. He'd just seemed happy to hear from her and keen to see her again. She was trying not to think about it.

The opening was at seven, so Cat had got changed at work – out of the wide-legged black trousers and white shirt she wore at least twice a week – and into skinny jeans, boots and an almost sheer bright-pink shirt over a white vest, and then headed down to The Jack Horner, the pub everyone went to if they went for a drink after work.

She drank two glasses of wine there, while playing a game on her phone – and intermittently checking in case Harvey had to cancel – and then grabbed a black cab outside to take her down to Carnaby Street.

She was nervous. Which seemed ridiculous. It wasn't a date, nothing was going to happen, it was just Harvey. And yet. It felt like a date. She wondered if Harvey thought it was a date. She'd have to tell him it wasn't. Definitely not. She'd suggested they meet at a nearby pub since Cat didn't know what the forest bar was going to be like, and it was only when Cat walked in she realised it was a pub she'd done stand-up in. They had a small room upstairs with only about eight tables. The floor was sticky and the windows were dirty, but it had been a good gig because... because it was the first time Sam had gone to see her perform.

She shouldn't be there. She shouldn't be there on a pretend date with Harvey. This was a really bad idea. She turned to leave, planning to text Harvey on the way to the Tube, but he was right there, smiling at her, a beanie on his head and a dimple in his cheek and Cat was screwed.

'Hey!' she said. 'You came!'

The pub was small but not cramped and they found seats in the corner near the fireplace. Harvey pulled his beanie off and tucked it into the pocket of his coat, before running a hand back through his hair.

'How was work?' Cat asked him, curling her hand around the stem of the glass of wine Harvey had got her. She'd better not have another in the next place. Three was plenty. Probably.

'Day off today,' Harvey said.

'What? But that was the whole point! That you were only across the road.'

And yet he'd come anyway, Cat thought.

'Well.' Harvey fiddled with the label on his bottle of beer. 'If I had been in work, I wouldn't have been able to come. Because I'd have been working.' He smiled.

'Oh,' Cat said. 'Oh yeah. I didn't think of that. So have you come far?' She hoped that didn't sound like she was angling to know where he lived. Even though she totally was.

'No, just Marylebone. It's like a fifteen-minute walk.'

'You live in Marylebone?' Cat asked.

He nodded, picking up his beer. 'It's not my place. I'm flat-sitting for a friend.'

'A rich friend?'

Harvey smiled. 'Pretty much, yeah.'

'Wow.'

They finished their drinks while Cat told Harvey just how much Arnold had been talking about him since the theatre tour.

'He asked me if we could go to every show,' Cat said.

'I mean, that could be arranged.' Harvey pulled his coat on and held Cat's fake leopard jacket out to her. She took it and shrugged it on and followed him out of the pub.

The launch wasn't hard to find. Two streets away and sign-posted by an enormous tree apparently growing out of the front of the building. Cat gave her name to the bouncer and he ticked her off a list, ushering the two of them inside.

'Woah,' Harvey said, shrugging off his coat again.

'So it really is a forest,' Cat said, passing her coat over into the cloakroom along with Harvey's.

The space was filled with trees, hung with lanterns and fairy lights, tables curling around their trunks. A fire pit ran down the centre of the room with metal buckets of marshmallows and toasting forks hanging from the sides. The bar at the far end was already rammed, but more buckets were dotted about, filled with ice and beers and Cat spotted a few people wandering around with trays of wine. She decided to have just one more glass.

Once they'd grabbed their drinks, they walked through the trees to a small clearing with armchairs and another, smaller, fire pit. They sat down and Harvey said, 'This place is mad.'

'Right? Arnold would love it actually. He loves trees and actually also fire. We're trying not to read anything into it.' She smiled.

'We?' Harvey frowned.

'Me and Kelly.'

'Right.' Harvey drank some of his beer. 'So Kelly helps you with him?'

Cat blinked. She was on her fourth glass of wine, yes, but she definitely seemed to be missing something.

'I help Kelly. When I can. And she's pregnant again and pretty sick, which is why...' Something slowly fell into place in her brain and it obviously occurred to Harvey at the same time because his eyes widened and even in the low light, Cat could see his cheeks had turned pink.

'He's not yours?' Harvey said at the same time as Cat said, 'You thought he was mine?'

'God, I'm so embarrassed,' Harvey said. 'You never said. And I just assumed—'

Cat shook her head. 'No, it's my fault. I should have said. I just didn't think.'

Cat drained the rest of her wine, as another realisation dawned. Harvey had thought that Arnold was her son. Her five-year-old son.

'So if you thought he was mine,' Cat said, 'does that mean you also thought...'

'Um,' Harvey said. 'Yeah.'

'But you didn't mention that to Sam, right?'

'No!' Harvey said. 'God. No. I haven't even told him that I've seen you. I mean, he knows you came to his show.'

'God,' Cat said.

The problem with being in a small clearing in a fake forest is that there was no one to top up your wine.

'And, ah, what did he think about that?'

'About you coming to the show?'

Cat nodded.

'He was pleased. I think? He said he wished you'd hung around. It would have been good to see you.'

'Right,' Cat said. 'OK. That's... thanks for telling me.'

'I really am sorry,' Harvey said.

'It's fine,' Cat told him.

But it wasn't, not really. They stayed a little longer, but they never managed to recover their earlier ease. Conversation was stilted and awkward, while Harvey repeatedly apologised and Cat tried not to think about Sam. Seeing Sam. Talking to Sam. And Harvey thinking that Arnold was Cat and Sam's kid.

It was the worst fake date she'd ever had.

CHAPTER FOURTEEN

Cat had woken up feeling like shit. Too much wine. Not enough food. And the awkward conversation and disappointing evening had put her in a filthy mood. There was no milk again and Georgie had left the kitchen in a complete mess, which made her feel even worse. And then she'd found a postcard her dad had sent and someone had tucked away down the side of the breadbin. All it said was 'Give us a call, eh?' but it made her feel guilty for not having called him back already and furious that she lived with people who didn't seem to have any sense of consideration at all.

She'd stopped for coffee on the way to work – getting an extra shot and a muffin for the sugar – and had announced to the office that she felt like shit and they should all keep away.

Fortunately, no one was that bothered. They all had their own work to do and Colin was over in the Soho Square office sorting shit out with Nick.

Cat finished the VAT Returns she'd been putting off, actually did come up with a way to streamline the invoicing, and was wondering about chasing some client accounts when the door buzzer went.

'There's a reception,' Cat said to no one.

'Not today,' Phil said from the desk behind Cat. 'Receptionist is off sick. There's a sign. Didn't you notice?'

Cat had actually been playing the dot game on her phone, so no, she hadn't noticed. And she was nearest to the door. Sighing, she got up and answered the entry phone.

'I'm, ah, looking for Cat Gardner?'

For a second, Cat thought it was Harvey and something fluttered in her chest. But then she realised.

'Sam?'

'Yeah. Is that you? Cat?'

'Yeah. This is me. I mean it's me, Cat. I'll buzz you up.'

Cat wanted to run to the bathroom to see how she looked but she knew there wasn't time. And she also knew she looked like crap. She hadn't had time to shower this morning because she'd woken from a dream where she was having a threesome with Harvey and Ariana Grande of all people and she'd spent the next half an hour trying to get back to sleep and, when that failed, trying to recreate the dream in her imagination. Also there was the whole 'feeling like shit' thing.

The door opened and there was Sam. For the first time in five years. Just... standing there.

'Hi,' Cat said.

He looked exactly the same. He was even wearing the same jacket: a black bomber Cat had spotted one day in Camden market. He had a long, dark red scarf wrapped around his neck and he unwound it while he glanced around the office.

Cat was already flustered enough to see Sam in her office and wasn't even going to think about the fact that he knew where to find her, that she was exactly where she'd been when he'd left. Her life hadn't moved on at all.

'Is everything OK?' Cat asked.

What if he'd come to tell her something had happened to someone. His mum. Or Harvey. Cat's stomach churned and she wanted to sit down. What if something had happened to Harvey? But then if something had happened to Harvey, Sam wouldn't come to see her. Because he didn't know she'd seen Harvey.

'Can we talk?' Sam asked. 'Like... is there somewhere...'

Cat shook her head. 'Let's go and get a coffee.'

She grabbed her coat off the hook next to the wall.

'I'm going out,' she told Phil. 'If Colin comes back…'

'No worries,' Phil said, without looking up.

Cat and Sam walked out of the building in silence.

'There's a place just at the end of the road,' Cat said.

The coffee shop was small and shabby but Cat had been there before and the coffee was decent. She got a latte for herself and an Americano for Sam without asking. She carried them both over to the side table and added sugar but no milk to his.

'You still take it the same, yeah?' she asked him, as she sat down, pushing his coffee across the table towards him.

He nodded. 'Thanks.'

Cat stared at him. She hadn't seen him for five years. Three years longer than they'd been together. He still looked the same. He looked good. But five years was a long time. She couldn't quite think of him as the man she'd fallen in love with, had really great sex with, the man she'd thought she might spend the rest of her life with until he'd fucked off to Australia and left her behind.

'So my mum is freaking out about something,' he said. 'And she told me and now I'm kind of freaking out too.'

'I haven't got a kid,' Cat said.

Sam's eyebrows shot up instantly. 'How did you—'

'Harvey didn't tell you?' Cat asked.

Sam shook his head. 'Tell me what?'

'He… I didn't realise he thought Arnold was mine. But I told him. Last night. He didn't—'

'You talked to Harvey last night?' He was turning his cup round and round on the table. Five years ago she would have reached out and stilled his hand, but she couldn't do that any more.

'We went to the launch of a bar. Just… we're friends. Sort of.'

Sam shook his head, his eyes narrowed in confusion.

'You and Harvey aren't…'

'No!' Cat said. 'God. No, of course not. I bumped into him at your… your gig. And then again in John Lewis when I was taking Arnold to the grotto. Arnold is Kelly's son. I didn't even realise Harvey thought anything else.'

'Mum said something about Harvey's theatre?'

'Yeah. When we bumped into him, he offered us – me and Arnold – panto tickets. I was going to give them to Kelly actually, but she's pregnant again and she's sick, so I took him. And then she was invited to this launch – she gets loads of free shit for her blog – and I invited Harvey cos it was near his theatre and as like a thank you cos he was so great with Arnold. Arnold's in love with him. And then he asked me about him – Harvey. Asked me about Arnold. I hadn't even thought that he might think…' She shook her head. 'And that's it.'

'Right,' Sam said. 'So he's Kelly's.'

'He's Kelly's.' Cat picked up her latte.

'Not yours.'

She shook her head. 'Not mine. And not yours.'

'Right,' Sam said. 'OK. Good. I didn't think that you would have—'

'I wouldn't,' Cat said. 'No way. There's no way I wouldn't have told you.'

'That's what Mum said. But we were both just… you know.'

'Yeah,' Cat said. She put her latte down again. Her hands were shaking. 'How did your mum even know about Arnold?'

'Harvey told her.'

Cat shook her head. 'Why would he—'

'I don't think he intended to. He was worried about it. I think he just wanted to know if she thought it was possible. And I'm sure he didn't expect her to tell me.'

'Right,' Cat said. She kind of wanted to strangle Harvey. She couldn't believe he hadn't told her last night that he'd got his mum all worked up too. But then that would've made it even more awkward than it already was.

'It's good to see you,' Sam said into his cup. 'I wanted to see you. When Harv said you came to my show.'

'Yeah,' Cat said. Her throat felt tight. She didn't trust herself to speak without crying. She'd thought she and Harvey were becoming friends. Apparently not.

'What did you think?' Sam sipped his coffee, winced, and then blew across the surface of the dark liquid.

'It was good,' she managed to squeak out.

'And you didn't mind that... you know?'

Cat sucked in a long breath. 'That it's about me? Part of it?' She shook her head. 'Your life's yours to write about. We agreed that.'

Sam nodded. 'I appreciate it.'

Cat drank some of her coffee, feeling it warm through her chest.

'How long are you back for?'

Sam shrugged. 'Indefinitely, I guess. I've got a few gigs set up.'

Cat blinked in surprise. She'd been assuming he was just back for gigs, not permanently.

'What happened to Australia?'

'It was great,' Sam said. 'It's been brilliant for me. I mean, I meant to stay a year and I stayed five. But I feel like a change of scene. And I miss the family. And just, you know, home.'

Cat nodded. It must be nice. To have a home to come back to. And a family. She had Kelly and Sean and Arnold, but it wasn't the same. They weren't really hers.

'What are you doing for Christmas?' Sam asked.

'At Kelly's. She's pregnant again. That one's not yours either.'

Sam laughed. 'That'll be nice.'

Cat nodded. It would be. It always was. 'Is your mum doing a whole...' She wafted her hand. Jan loved Christmas and prepared for it months in advance. The one Christmas Cat had spent with them had been one of the best of her life. Seemingly endless mince pies and wine, party games, evening walks in the freezing cold air, everyone laughing and just… loving each other. It made Cat's heart hurt to remember it.

'Course she is.' They smiled at each other. 'Harvey said you're gigging again,' Sam said.

Cat smothered a groan. Why had she said that? She had no intention of doing stand-up again. She hadn't wanted to do it since Sam had left.

'I'm not,' Cat said. 'It's just something I was—'

'You should,' Sam said. 'You were good. I can't believe you ever stopped.'

Cat looked down at her hands curled around her coffee. She wanted to ask Sam why he'd left. Why he hadn't asked her to go with him. Was she so easy to just walk away from?

Instead she said, 'It just wasn't fun for me any more.'

Once they'd finished their coffees, they walked back towards the office and Cat thought about how surreal it was that she couldn't reach out and take his hand like she would've done in the past. How they used to be in love and now they were basically strangers.

'Sorry again,' Sam said, standing outside Cat's building. 'I shouldn't have—'

'It's OK,' Cat said. 'Obviously you'd want to know if…'

'Yeah.'

They stared at each other.

'Can I ask you something?' Cat said.

Sam nodded. 'Course.'

'Am I a cat or a pigeon?'

Sam let out a bark of laughter. 'Seriously?'

'Seriously!' Cat said. She wanted to shove him. 'I don't think either of them fit me so I was confused.'

Sam laughed again, rubbing one hand over his mouth. 'I mean, if neither of them fit, maybe you're neither.'

'Come on,' Cat said, shaking her head.

'I think you know which one you are,' Sam said.

'You're the one that flew away,' Cat said. 'Not me.'

She pictured him packing as she hid in the bathroom, crying.

Sam shrugged. 'There's more than one way to fly away.'

CHAPTER FIFTEEN

'What was it like,' Kelly asked, 'seeing him again?'

Cat shook her head. 'Kind of… surreal. Like, it's been so long. And I was looking at him and he looked the same, but we don't know each other. Like… I used to put his willy in my mouth, you know?'

'Oh, I know,' Kelly said. 'You didn't, right? Yesterday.'

Cat snorted. 'No. It would've been weird. But also I feel like maybe it wouldn't be. If I'd asked and he'd said yes, we could go straight back there.'

'You mean you wanted to? You thought about it?'

'No. I mean I thought about it, because that's what I do. But I wasn't, like, attracted to him. Even though he looks good. It was more just like… we used to do that and we probably could again.'

'Right,' Kelly said. 'I think I see.'

Cat shrugged. 'I don't know. It was mostly surreal, like I said. Like he genuinely thought I'd had his kid and just not mentioned it for five years.'

'It happens,' Kelly said.

'But I would never! And surely he knows that. He definitely used to know that. Know me well enough to know that.'

'Right. But you can also see why he might think that,' Kelly said. 'Like if it was the other way round, you'd think it, I know you would.'

Cat sniffed. 'Yeah. But I've got an overactive imagination.'

She picked at the bowl of crisps Kelly had set out on the coffee table. Kelly was dipping hers into a milkshake Sean had brought her from McDonald's on his way back from work.

'He didn't seem keen on the idea of me seeing Harvey,' Cat said, crunching.

'No shit,' Kelly said.

'As if it's got anything to do with him.'

'I mean, he is literally the reason you won't consider going out with Harvey.'

Cat dropped her head back against the sofa and groaned. 'Why is it all so stressful?'

'What?'

'Life! I just... why can't I be you? Lovely calm house with a lovely calm husband and an occasionally calm, but always adorable child? Why do I have to love people who just fuck off. And then either don't come back or come back asking stupid fucking questions.'

'You love me and I've never fucked off,' Kelly said.

Cat shuffled along the sofa and rested her head on her friend's shoulder. 'And I love that about you.'

'You did try to make me,' Kelly said.

'I know,' Cat said quietly.

'I think sometimes you try to push people away before they can leave you.'

It wasn't the first time they'd had this conversation, but it was the first time for a while. The very first time had been after Sam had left and Kelly had suggested that Cat could have told him she wanted to go to Australia with him. It had led to the biggest row of their friendship and to Cat moving out of Kelly and Sean's house and into the flat with Georgie. She'd always regretted it.

'I don't think I pushed Sam away,' Cat said. 'Did I?'

Kelly kissed her friend's temple. 'Why don't you ask him?'

'Ugh, no. He thinks I'm a pigeon. A pigeon who had his kid and hid it for five years. I've never seen a baby pigeon, have you?'

'You're both idiots,' Kelly said.

Cat didn't want to talk to Sam again. She did want to talk to Harvey though. She wanted to ask him why he'd told Jan before mentioning it to her. But so far she'd been too pissed off to even text him. Maybe she should copy her dad and send him a postcard.

'I think I can help with the stress,' Kelly said.

'Wow.' Cat snuggled further into her side. 'You know I don't love you that way.'

'Shut up,' Kelly said, shoving her. 'I've been offered a review trip to a spa.'

'Spar?' Cat said. 'Good selection of milk. Sometimes the apples are a bit brown.'

Kelly rolled her eyes. 'Saunas, hydrotherapy pool, massage. All that stuff. I can't go cos pregnant and feel like shit, so I thought you might want to do it.'

'What would I have to do?'

'Just sample the treatments, make a few notes, tell me about it when you get back and then either you can write the blog post or I can. The company has spas and hotels all over, so it's worth doing. If they like the post, they'll offer more and you could always do them too.'

'Sounds good. What's the catch?'

'You'd need to take a man.'

'Oh, just that one small detail!' Cat said. 'Not a problem. There are men everywhere! Just this morning, I sat next to one on the Tube. He was wearing a T-shirt with tits on it and spent the entire journey clearing his throat and coughing into a hanky, but I'm sure he'd be a delightful companion at a fancy spa.'

'Wow,' Kelly said.

'Could I take Sean?'

'No.'

'Scared he won't be able to resist my charms?'

'I know for a fact that he's terrified of your charms. And also no, I need him here. Cos sick and pregnant.'

'Hmm. Who then?'

Kelly grinned. 'Nick?'

'Brilliant. "Hey, gay co-worker who I awkwardly asked out, fancy getting naked and rubbed with oils with me?"'

'Well, it's a couple's spa day. I mean, you could take a woman, but I don't know if you're up to pretending to be gay for a day.'

'I could rock it,' Cat said. 'If I could think of anyone to take.'

'I know who you could take,' Kelly said.

'Don't say Sam. The blow job thing was purely theoretical.'

Kelly just stared at her, one eyebrow raised.

'Seriously?' Cat said. 'The last time I saw him it was incredibly awkward. And that was before I knew he'd told his mum I had Sam's love child.'

'And you haven't heard from him?'

'He texted. To apologise again.'

'And you replied?'

Cat shrugged. 'That it was fine. I mean, what am I going to say? That it really pissed me off? That I can't believe he did it?'

'You could say that,' Kelly said. 'You know, instead of just internally stewing.'

'What's the point?' Cat said.

Kelly shook her head. 'The point is that it's good to tell people how you feel, get things off your chest, clear the air!'

'I could do that,' Cat said. 'Or I could just... not do that.'

'You wouldn't need to stay over,' Kelly said, ignoring her. 'You could use the facilities, get a massage or whatever – and, no, it doesn't have to be a sexy massage – have dinner and drinks, and then have the option to stay over if things were going well. Also you'll have all day to tell him how pissed off you are.'

'Jesus,' Cat said. She pictured herself and Harvey in the hotel on Kelly's screen. Lounging on the huge squashy sofas. Drinking champagne on the terrace overlooking the grounds. Shagging madly up against the sliding glass doors of the enormous shower. She shifted on the sofa.

'Are you humping my cushions?' Kelly asked.

'No.' She picked up a cushion and cuddled it against her stomach. 'I don't know though. What if he said no.'

'What if he said yes? I mean, what have you got to lose? Apart from your two-year no-sex streak.'

'I'll think about it,' Cat said. But there was no way she was actually going to ask him. No way.

CHAPTER SIXTEEN

Cat could hear the noises from the stairs. Sex noises. Sex noises coming from her flat. Unless the wanking guy had got himself a girlfriend and maybe learned ventriloquism at the same time. No, it was definitely her flat. She pushed open the front door and was immediately confronted with the sight of a hairy arse going up and down on her sofa. She pulled the door closed again, shuddering.

She'd been looking forward to getting home. She'd planned to have a bath, cook a pizza, get into bed and watch something mindless on Netflix. This was why she spent so much time at Kelly's. But it was also why it wasn't ideal. She shouldn't feel so unwelcome in her own home. And she knew from experience that if she mentioned it to Georgie, Georgie would call her a prude and insinuate (mostly with an eyebrow, but still) that it was because Cat never got to have any sex herself.

Cat almost ran back down the stairs and out into the street. Her phone was vibrating in her pocket, but she ignored it. She needed a drink. Today had been a lot and she wasn't prepared to deal with another single thing until she had some alcohol in her system.

The nearest bar to Cat's flat was an absolute shithole. The next one – only about five minutes' walk away – was lovely: small and cosy, but with the seating well-spaced enough so as to not be claustrophobic. Plus there was a fireplace. Cat unwound her scarf, hung her chilled coat on the back of her seat and went to the bar for a glass of red. Only when she was curled up in her chair and her fingers had unfrozen did she check her phone.

And found she had a voicemail notification. She knew it was her dad. Well. She didn't know it was him. But she was fairly confident. No one else left her voicemails. Of course, it could be someone wanting to discuss an accident that wasn't her fault. Or a wrong number. But it was definitely her dad. She could feel it.

She tucked one leg up under her and leaned back in the chair, still staring at the screen. What would Kelly do? Cat had that thought so often that she should get it tattooed: WWKD. Kelly would listen to it straight away. She certainly wouldn't sit staring at it and getting in a state about what it might be. She would grab the bull by the balls – wait, no, horn. Was that better? It was still grabbing a bull by something a bull wouldn't want to be grabbed by. But maybe that was the point of the expression. Cat picked up her phone and had got as far as typing 'grab the bull by...' into Google before she remembered she wasn't meant to be learning the etymology of idioms; she was meant to be acting like an adult and listening to the voicemail from her dad.

She took a deep breath, tapped on the voicemail icon, and held the speaker up to her ear.

'Catherine? Cat? It's your dad. I'm in London for a few days and I'd love to see you. Call me on this number, yeah?'

He had a slight Australian accent, she thought. She'd never noticed that before. Something had changed since the last time she'd spoken to him anyway. He was doing that thing where his voice went up at the end of each sentence. Like people complained about teenage girls. In fact, she thought she remembered him complaining about it when she was a teenage girl (who watched too much *Neighbours*). Weird.

She couldn't think how long it was since she'd last seen him. It was at least a year. Where had they gone? There was a time when they'd sat outside a pub in Camden and he'd kept looking at his Apple Watch until she'd wanted to rip it off his wrist and throw it into the canal. How long had Apple Watches been around? Not more than a couple of years?

Afterwards, she'd bought a bottle of vodka from the wine shop on the corner and had apparently phoned Kelly, weeping, in the early hours. She'd woken up the next morning in her room – the spare room – at Kelly's and, after vomiting into the bowl Kelly had left next to the bed (and drinking the water and taking the paracetamol Kelly had left on the bedside table), she'd vaguely remembered lying in the back of Kelly's car, weeping, as the orangey light from the street lamps shuttled past the windows. The rest had been pretty much a blank.

'I think you should see a counsellor,' Kelly had told her the following morning, over a full cooked breakfast.

And even though Cat had argued that she didn't need to, that it was just seeing her dad set something off in her, but he was on his way back to Australia and she probably wouldn't see him for at least a couple of years and she could ignore his calls no problem, basically happily pretend he didn't exist, Kelly hadn't seemed to think that was a particularly healthy way of dealing with it and had said some other stuff that had made Cat cry and feel guilty and so she'd arranged a trial appointment with a counsellor she found online. The website had said it was free, but the counsellor asked for thirty quid and Cat paid it, so she had already felt pretty resentful before she even met the woman.

And it was fine. It had all been a bit awkward and embarrassing. The woman – her name was Jen – worked from the front room of her own house and the whole time they were talking, Cat could hear her dogs (she had three King Charles spaniels, if the framed photos on the mantlepiece were up to date) barking in another room. She'd made Cat Earl Grey tea in a china mug and left it on the side table next to her, along with a packet of tissues.

'People often find they need them,' she'd told Cat.

Cat had wanted to make a joke about it not being the time or place for a wank, but she managed to restrain herself, which was actually progress. Maybe counselling was working already.

'So,' Jen had said, sitting on a dining chair diagonally across the room. 'Why are you here?'

'Because my best friend told me I should come,' Cat said. She knew it was the wrong answer. But also that was why she was there and she'd told herself she should at least try to be honest.

'And why does she think you need to come?'

Cat bit at her lips. 'Because my dad came to visit and I got shitfa— drunk.'

'And why do you think you did that?' Jen asked. And Cat decided she was wasting her time. Her time and Jen's time.

'Because he left,' she said. And then she told Jen the basic story – the same story she told everyone – but she wasn't really paying attention. She was looking at the carpet, the fireplace, the curtains, the pictures on the walls. Even Jen's black leather diary, open on the coffee table, ready for her to book Cat in for another appointment. But Cat already knew there wouldn't be another appointment. She knew what her issue with her dad was; she didn't need to shell out her hard-earned cash to talk about it with a stranger.

'When your father left,' Jen said – she'd been sitting with her legs crossed, but now her feet were flat on the floor and she leaned forward to focus more intently on Cat, 'what did your mother do?'

Cat's breath caught in her chest. She reached for the tea, but her hands were shaking. And she hated Earl Grey anyway; it tasted like perfume.

'What do you mean, do?' she asked instead.

'Did she talk to you about it at all?'

'She told me that he'd gone. And why.'

'What reason did she give?'

'What do you mean?' Cat said again.

'You said she told you why he'd gone.'

'She said he wasn't happy. And he wanted to…' What had she said? Cat knew her mum had told her something; she must have done. But she couldn't think. 'He wanted to…' Cat shook her head. 'I can't…'

'It's OK,' Jen said. 'We can come back to that.'

Now, in the pub, Cat texted her dad and said she wasn't going to be around, sorry. Then she deleted the voicemail so she wasn't tempted to listen to it over and over in the middle of the night when her resistance was low. She finished her wine, wrapped herself back up, and headed home.

CHAPTER SEVENTEEN

Cat blamed her emotionally fraught day for what happened when she got back to her flat. Georgie and her boyfriend had gone out, but they'd actually left a used condom on the coffee table. Cat had stared at it for a while, something like fury building behind her breastbone, before she'd heated the pizza, retrieved her beer from its hiding place in a bag of carrots at the back of the salad tray, and crawled into bed. And it was there that her phone had rung. And it wasn't her dad. It was Harvey.

'I'm starting to think you're avoiding me,' he said.

Cat could hear the smile in his voice, but also a nervousness too – he wasn't sure how pissed off she was.

'I'm not…' Cat started. And then stopped herself. 'Yeah. A bit. Sorry. I just… I don't understand why you told your mum.'

'I didn't mean to!' Harvey said. 'I couldn't stop thinking about it. And I didn't think you would have done that. Not without telling Sam. So I gave my mum a hypothetical and she just kind of weaselled it out of me. I told her not to tell Sam. I still can't believe she did.'

'Right,' Cat said.

She folded some pizza into her mouth and pulled the duvet up to her chin. She was still fully dressed but she could sort that out later. Or sleep in her clothes. Either one.

'I shouldn't have said anything,' Harvey said. 'To Mum, I mean. Before I spoke to you.'

'No,' Cat said. 'You really shouldn't have. But… no harm done, I guess.'

'Was Sam…'

'He was fine,' Cat said. 'It went about as well as those ex-boyfriend turning up at your work to accuse you of hiding a secret kid things always go.'

'Shit,' Harvey said. 'I really am sorry.'

Cat shrugged before realising he couldn't see her. 'Doesn't matter. Honestly. I've had quite a day. It's the least of my problems.'

'Want to talk about it?' Harvey asked.

'Nah,' Cat said. But then she told him everything anyway. How one of the other account managers had fucked up a tax return and Colin had asked Cat to sort it out, which pissed off the original manager and also meant that Cat got yelled at by the client. And then there was the call from her dad, which she didn't mention. And the sex on the sofa and condom on the coffee table, which she did.

'Shit,' Harvey said. 'That is not a good day.'

'That's not even all of it,' Cat said. 'They were the edited highlights.'

'I think you need to talk to your roommates…' Harvey said gently.

'I was thinking maybe a passive aggressive note,' Cat said.

Harvey laughed. 'That could work. But I always think talking is better.'

'Yeah, you're probably right,' Cat said. 'Or maybe I'll just move out.'

'That sounds like a good idea.'

'But where would I go? I've had a look at places I can afford and Kelly's got cupboards that look more comfortable. Actually I probably could move into one of Kelly's cupboards.'

'I know,' Harvey said. 'It's shitty. I'm sorry.'

Cat felt her shoulders start to relax for the first time in years. She shuffled down further under the duvet and thought about how sweet Harvey had been with Arnold. How well they'd got on in the first pub before the awkwardness of the conversation in the fake forest.

'I wanted to ask you something actually,' Cat said, closing her eyes as if she could hide from herself. 'It's going to sound a bit weird.'

Oh god, now she'd made it sound like she was about to Pretty Woman him. 'It's not sex or anything.' Yeah, that was definitely less awkward.

Harvey laughed. 'I didn't think it was. I do now, obviously.'

'God. Shut up. OK, you know Kelly? And her blog? She gets all these press opportunities and she's offered me one at a spa – you know, massages, steam rooms, watercress and melon for lunch? But it's for couples, so I have to take a man. And I don't know any. But I really want to go because I'm stressed to fuck. So. What do you think?'

There was another silence, which Cat filled by assuming Harvey was appalled at the idea and wondering how he could leave the country and change his identity.

'I mean, that's not the most flattering offer I've ever had,' he said eventually.

Cat laughed. 'I'm sorry. What I meant was, I think it would be nice to spend a day at a spa with you. What do you think?'

'I think it sounds great,' Harvey said. 'I'd love to join you. For massages, steam rooms, and shit salad. Thank you.'

'Great,' Cat said. 'Text me your email and I'll send you the info.'

'And just so you know?' he added. 'If you had been propositioning me? I'd have been fine with that.'

Cat hadn't long ended the call and was trying to decide between a bath and bed, when there was a tentative knock on her door and Georgie popped her head round.

'Got a minute?'

Cat shuffled up to lean back against the headboard. 'I actually wanted to talk to you too.'

Georgie sat at the end of Cat's bed, pulling her feet up to sit cross-legged and picking the yellow polish off her toenails as she talked.

'So I don't know if you know that this flat was for sale,' Georgie started.

Cat blinked at her. 'No. I had no idea. Since when?'

'Not long actually,' Georgie said. 'But now it's sold.'

'It's sold?!' Cat said. 'Shit. What does that mean?'

'Well, the thing is—' Georgie stretched one leg out to the side '—we've bought it.'

For a second, Cat thought she meant the two of them: Georgie and Cat. She felt a burst of relief to be secure, to have a home that couldn't be snatched away on a whim, to not have to constantly cull her possessions because it was too much of a faff (and too expensive) to hire a van to move each time. She hadn't exactly planned to go into home ownership with someone she couldn't really stand, but swings and roundabouts.

And then she realised.

'You mean you have. You and...' She was totally blanking on Georgie's boyfriend's name.

'Pete,' Georgie filled in. 'Yes.'

'Right,' Cat said.

'So I guess this is me giving you six weeks' notice to leave.'

'Right,' Cat said again. 'OK. Thanks for letting me know.'

Of course she was going to let her know. She wanted her out. In six weeks! Cat had no idea where she was going to go.

Georgie stood up and headed back over to the door, stopping with her hand on the handle.

'Oh, what did you want to talk to me about?'

Cat shook her head. 'It doesn't matter now.'

CHAPTER EIGHTEEN

'So,' Nick said from the other side of the table. 'Good Christmas?'

He'd texted her and suggested they meet in Central London, away from the office. They'd met at Picturehouse Central, upstairs in the members' bar, with a view of Shaftesbury Avenue that reminded Cat of why she loved London so much. Sometimes.

She'd seen Nick at work a few times since the embarrassing incident, and they seemed to have got past it fairly well – Cat only blushed approximately three shades darker than her natural tone by now – but the last time he'd come in, he'd suggested that they actually go and get the coffee and here they were.

'Yeah. Lovely, thanks.' She'd spent Christmas Day and Boxing Day at Kelly's and the rest of the week sorting through her belongings to see what she needed to pack and what she could throw away. It wasn't the most fun she'd ever had. 'You?'

'Great, thanks. I went to Mexico.'

'Of course you did,' she said. She'd noticed he was looking tanned when she'd first arrived, but assumed it was fake.

'So,' he said, sitting back in his seat and half-smiling at her. 'I'm moving to the New York office.'

'Yes,' Cat agreed. She didn't want to think about it. She picked up her drink and took a sip.

'And I was wondering if you wanted to come too,' Nick added.

Cat swallowed – he was lucky she hadn't done a spit-take – and stared at him. Her stomach had lurched at his words, but she'd almost certainly misheard. 'Sorry,' she said. 'Say that again?'

He leaned forward, grinning. 'You're the most efficient person in that office. More than Colin even. You stay calm under pressure, you're good with the clients, you don't make mistakes. I think you'd be an enormous asset to the New York office.'

Cat blew out a breath. 'Are you serious?'

'Absolutely. Also I'm a bit scared and I want a friend with me.' He grinned.

Cat laughed. 'God, Nick, that's—'

'Obviously, I don't expect you to decide straight away. Think about it. Talk to your friends and your… imaginary boyfriend. And then once I'm out there, you can come out for a few days and see what you think. No pressure. I'll email you the package – it's better money. And relocation would be covered, obviously.'

'Obviously,' Cat said faintly.

'There's plenty of stand-up clubs too,' Nick said, smiling.

The thought of doing stand-up in New York was terrifying, but also there was a flicker of excitement deep down that Cat hadn't felt for a while.

'And I wanted to ask you something else,' Nick said. 'Will you do stand-up at my leaving do?'

'God,' Cat said, her head spinning. 'Yeah. Of course.'

Cat couldn't face going back to the office. She'd told Colin she had a doctor's appointment and, after leaving Nick, she called and said she was having to go to the hospital for tests. Instead she crossed over Shaftesbury Avenue and just started walking, her coat pulled tight around her.

New York.

She'd always thought it would be amazing to live there. And she could start a whole new life. She'd miss Kelly. Obviously. But that might be for the best. She knew she was too dependent on her. And Kelly was going to be too busy to take care of Cat along with two kids. And really wasn't it time Cat should be taking care of herself? As long as she had Kelly to bail her out, as long as she could run away to Kelly's whenever something went wrong, how was she ever going to learn to stand on her own two feet? How could she ever actually grow up? And she needed to find a new flat anyway. Why shouldn't it be in New York? The timing was perfect.

Standing on the corner of Brewer Street she was hit by a pang of grief so strong that she bent double. She tried not to think about her mum too much or too often. Whenever something reminded Cat of her – a song on the radio, the scent of the Trésor perfume she always asked for for Christmas and birthdays, even something stupid sometimes like the texture of a fabric or the sound of a spoon in a cup of tea – Cat pushed it away and thought about something else instead. She was scared that if she let herself properly think about it, it would destroy her. But standing on the corner of Brewer Street, she felt totally alone in a way she hadn't for a long time.

She took a breath, looked both ways, and crossed. As she skirted Golden Square, she told herself it was a good thing. She was entirely responsible for her own life. She could do whatever she wanted. She was only limited by her imagination. And the fact that she had about seventeen quid in the bank. But if she did decide to go to New York, all of that could change.

She and Kelly had gone to New York together after university. The first weekend in July so they'd expected – and packed for – sun. It rained every single day. Cat's best memory was of the two of them running across Broadway, rain streaming down their faces and splashing up their legs, the lights from the shops and neon signs reflected in the water on the ground. A couple of firefighters had been standing outside their firehouse and cheered when Cat had lurched into a particularly deep puddle, and by the time the two of them made it into the Starbucks they were aiming for (one of four within two minutes of their hotel), they were as soaked as if they'd just got out of the shower.

Now she pictured herself living there. Working there. Going to bars and making friends and meeting people and having an entirely different life.

Her phone started vibrating again. It was probably her dad. He'd left another message a couple of days ago, but Cat hadn't called him back yet. She still hadn't decided if she was going to call him back at all.

Cat walked up Carnaby Street, stopping every couple of minutes to tip her head back and look up at the Christmas lights. They were completely over the top: red, silver and green, shimmering and vibrating in the breeze. Cat loved them. But they'd be gone soon. And maybe she could be too.

Her hands were freezing, so she stopped at Pret for a coffee. And it was only when she stepped back outside that she realised where she was. John Lewis.

Where she'd brought Arnold to see Santa and they'd found Harvey instead.

If she went to New York, she could stop thinking about Harvey. She wouldn't have to see her dad, could stop thinking about everything. Leave it all behind. A blank slate. A fresh start.

But first she had to do stand-up at Nick's leaving do. Why the fuck had she agreed to *that*?

CHAPTER NINETEEN

The spa was on a main road, which surprised Cat, but as soon as she was inside, all thoughts of traffic went out of her head. It was like walking into a hotel. Perhaps in Morocco. Not that she'd been to Morocco. But the walls were cream marble (possibly not actually marble, but they looked like marble), the tiled floor made Cat immediately think of Instagram (#ihavethisthingwithfloors) and the furniture was huge and soft and jewel-coloured, red, blue, jade green. It smelled incredible too. Like flowers and the sea and something herbal. The contrast to the grey damp January day outside was startling.

'This is not what I was expecting,' Harvey whispered, from behind her.

It was so quiet and serene that Cat couldn't really imagine conducting a proper conversation there. She smiled at him over her shoulder and then checked them in at an enormous curved desk with a waterfall behind it. The receptionist directed all her questions to Harvey, even though Cat was the one answering them.

'She was flirting with you,' Cat told him as they headed to the changing rooms.

'She wasn't,' Harvey said. 'She was just being nice.'

Cat snorted and then covered her mouth when it echoed through the marble foyer.

'Smooth,' Harvey said.

'Shut it. We need to go and get changed.'

'I know,' Harvey said, smirking. 'Jasmine said the changing rooms are just over here to the left.'

'Jasmine.' Cat rolled her eyes. 'Bet her real name's Jane.'

'You're probably right, Catherine.'

'Oh my god.'

They'd reached the changing room doors and Cat said a small silent prayer that they weren't mixed. And it worked. Once through the main doors they were faced with separate changing rooms.

'See you on the other side,' Harvey said, pushing through the door with his shoulder.

Cat had a vision of them walking out through the verruca footbath and into an enormous chlorinated public pool, but of course that wasn't the case. She changed into her swimming costume ('plain but a bit sexy', Kelly had called it) in the stylish and calm changing rooms and then walked through to the stylish and calm spa.

Harvey was there already, sitting at a foot bath with his back to her, his white towelling robe hanging down behind him. It was only when Cat walked round to the opposite side, ready to sit down, that she saw his robe was open.

'No,' she said before she could stop herself.

'No what?' Harvey said.

She forced herself to look at his face and not his body. 'No, I don't want a foot spa.'

'It's good,' Harvey said. 'Bubbly.'

Cat sat down and lowered her feet into the water. It was indeed bubbly.

The foot spas were arranged around a central table so the two of them were sitting opposite each other, flat rock between them.

'I feel like we should be playing chess,' Harvey said.

'Do you play chess?'

Harvey shook his head. 'I'm more of a Scrabble man.'

'I think we should arm wrestle,' Cat said.

'Winner buys dinner?'

Cat put her elbow down on the table. 'Sounds like a plan.'

Harvey grinned and reached for her hand. Which was when she realised she hadn't thought this through. His hand was soft and huge and gripped hers firmly. She remembered how she'd held onto his hand at the theatre when they were encouraging Arnold to come out onto the light rigging. How it had made her feel safe.

'No cheating,' she said.

'Of course. Ready?'

She tried to relax her shoulders and firm her core and not be distracted by the Jacuzzi at her feet.

'Go.'

Cat had half-expected Harvey to just slam her arm right down, but whether he was lulling her into a false sense of security or whether all the bags of supermarket shopping she'd carried up to her flat had paid off, she managed to hold him at bay for a few seconds until her arm started to dip. She stared at their hands, releasing her fingers and adjusting her grip a little before pushing back. Harvey laughed and she looked at his face to see he was biting his lower lip, a frown line of concentration between his eyebrows. She pushed harder and actually managed to lower his arm a couple of inches before he flexed his hand and pushed their arms flat on the table.

'Shit,' Cat said.

'Guess I'm buying you dinner.'

'I've never been on a water bed,' Harvey said a couple of hours later.

They'd had breakfast in the courtyard garden, then split up to try out the various steam rooms. Cat had tried the Herbal Room, a 'Tropical' shower, the Menthol Room, and the Turkish Hammam (the air in that one was like a physical presence, as was the hairy bloke sitting in the corner, and she was dripping with sweat after just a couple of minutes). She'd showered again, popped into the ice room to cool down and that was where she'd found Harvey. He was sitting on the ice bench in just his shorts, long legs stretched out in front of him, head tipped back and eyes closed. Cat couldn't understand it. She could barely stand on the ice floor; the thought of sitting down on the bench was horrifying. She'd let her eyes drift down Harvey's body, wondering if the thought of straddling him on the bench would warm her up, and when her eyes returned to his face, he was looking at her with a small smile.

'Now I know why Pingu was always so pissed off,' she'd said.

They were sitting on sunloungers overlooking a hydrotherapy pool that seemed to be a swimming version of a treadmill: small with jets so she was effectively swimming on the spot.

'Well, no,' Cat replied. 'Because we're not swingers and it's not the seventies.'

'I'm going to try it,' Harvey said. 'Come on.'

'I'm staying here.' Cat closed her eyes and then felt Harvey's hand on her ankle, lifting her leg. She yelped and pulled it away. 'What are you doing?'

'Come on! Water bed! Live a little!'

'How is that living? Even a little?'

'Don't you need to review it? Think of all the jokes you could make about a water bed.'

'You make a good point,' Cat said, pulling her robe around herself and clambering off the sunlounger.

The water bed was unbelievably comfortable. Like lying on a cloud. A warm cloud that cradled and hugged in all the right places.

'This must be what Heaven is like,' Cat mumbled, her face squashed into the pillow.

'The gay club?' Harvey asked and Cat snorted again, opening one eye to look at him. He was looking back at her and he was too close, she had to close her eyes again.

'You're allowed to sleep, right?' Cat asked.

'I think we can do what we want as long as we're off them in forty-five minutes,' Harvey said.

That put some thoughts in Cat's head. She rolled onto her other side so Harvey didn't see her blush. She was trying to stop herself thinking about exactly what she could do with Harvey on a waterbed for forty-five minutes when she fell asleep.

'So where are we having dinner?' Harvey said.

They were dressed again and even though Harvey looked really bloody good in a long-sleeved grey jumper and a navy coat, Cat found she was disappointed he was wearing clothes. That was probably a bad sign. Although he did look good out of them.

'Tonight?' Cat asked.

'Unless you've got other plans?' Harvey said. 'Sorry, I didn't even think, I—'

'No,' Cat said. 'Tonight's fine. Tonight's good.'

'I thought we could walk up to this place I know in Marylebone,' Harvey said. 'Be about ten minutes' walk?'

'Sounds good.' Cat pulled her coat a little tighter around herself.

'Freezing, right?' Harvey said.

He pulled a black beanie out of his pocket and put it on, pulling it low on his forehead. It suited him.

'At least it's not snowing,' Cat said, as they started walking.

'It's meant to snow tomorrow, I think,' Harvey said. 'Or maybe next week?'

'Ugh,' Cat said.

'You don't like snow?' Harvey turned to look at her, his eyebrows pulled together.

'No? It's cold and wet and it fucks up the Tube and makes me late for work.'

'All fair points,' Harvey said. 'But consider this: it's magic.'

Cat laughed. 'Is it fuck.'

They stopped at a pedestrian crossing and Cat's phone started ringing.

'Sorry,' she said, pulling it out of her pocket and rejecting the call.

'You could have got that,' Harvey said. 'I don't mind.'

Cat shook her head. 'It's my dad. He's called a lot and I haven't decided what I want to say to him yet so I've just been, sort of, ignoring him.'

'Healthy,' Harvey said.

'I know.'

The lights changed and they started to cross.

'Sorry,' Harvey said. 'I didn't mean to intrud—'

'No, it's fine. I just… I don't really want to talk about him, if that's OK?'

'Course,' Harvey said. 'Sorry.'

Cat reached for his arm and squeezed it quickly, just above the elbow. 'It's OK, really. Sorry if I sounded snotty.'

'You didn't. I know families can be tricky.'

He obviously realised what he'd alluded to just as he said it and made a small groaning sound.

Cat laughed. 'Yeah, I think we should keep that subject off the table.'

They walked in silence for a while and Cat tried to think what Sam would say if he knew she was out with Harvey. If he knew they'd spent the day together and were going out to dinner. Nothing was going to happen between them, Cat knew that, but she didn't think Sam would like it anyway. She wouldn't. If it was her.

'It's just here,' Harvey said a little later, pointing at a small, cosy-looking restaurant on the corner. Cat followed him inside, unbuttoning her coat.

'Harvey!' A waiter – short and cute with closely shaved hair and a wide smile – crossed the room towards them.

'Hey!' Harvey said, beaming. 'Good to see you.'

'Where've you been?' the waiter asked. 'It's been too long.'

'Busy with work,' Harvey said. He turned and took Cat's coat, hanging it up on a coat stand just inside the door. 'This is Cat. Cat, this is Charlie.'

'Great to meet you,' Charlie said. 'Usual table?'

Cat followed the two of them across the room to a table in the far corner, under a mirror festooned with stickers, flyers, and fake flowers.

Harvey pulled Cat's chair out for her and she sat down with her back to the rest of the room.

'Is this OK?' Harvey asked her. 'The food's really great.'

'Can I get you drinks first?' Charlie asked.

Charlie and Harvey chatted while Cat looked at the menu and then ordered a glass of red.

'I was going to get red too,' Harvey said. 'Want to split a bottle?'

CHAPTER TWENTY

By the time the starters had arrived, Cat had downed a full glass and laughed so hard that she'd spat a bit of bread at Harvey. He hadn't even flinched as he'd brushed it off the table, grinning at her, chewing his own bit of bread roll. He looked sexy when he smiled and chewed, Cat didn't know why – it should be disgusting, like talking with your mouth full, but it wasn't.

'Is this your "first date" restaurant then?' Cat asked, cutting into her scallops. She almost hadn't ordered them because she'd read somewhere that scallops and pea puree was 'basic' but fuck it, she liked them and she'd never cook them at home cos she was scared of poisoning herself. Also, she didn't know how to puree a pea. 'Not that I'm saying this is a date. I know it's not a date.'

Harvey had the decency to look a little shamefaced. 'It's not, like, a thing. But I did used to come here with my ex-girlfriend a bit, yeah. She lived on a mews off Marylebone Road.'

'Blimey!' Cat said. 'Was she a princess?'

'She was, um, quite posh, yeah.'

'Bloody hell.' Cat shook her head. 'I live in Queen's Park… for now at least. I'm not posh.'

'I know,' Harvey said. 'But you're nice. She was horrible.'

'To you?' Cat couldn't imagine it.

Harvey nodded. 'Yep. Not at first. Well. A bit. I mean, she could be really great. But then she'd be awful. And then she was awful more than she was great. And then she slept with one of my friends, so.' He shrugged.

'I'm sorry,' Cat said.

'What about you? When was your last, um…'

They both realised at the same time that this probably was another conversational avenue they couldn't go down.

'Does he know we're here?' Cat asked. 'Did you tell him you were seeing me?'

Harvey shook his head. 'I've learned my lesson on telling my family stuff.'

Cat smiled. 'I don't know what to say. About Sam. I mean, I don't think he'd like it? If he knew we were…' She shook her head. 'Actually, that's just cos I wouldn't. I mean, I haven't got a sister, but if Kelly and Sean split – which will never happen; they're like the Posh and Becks of Crouch End – but if they did, and Kelly started going out with Sam… I don't know, man.'

'We're not "going out" though,' Harvey said, topping up Cat's glass. 'We're just having dinner. I think that's allowed.'

'I wouldn't want Sam to go out for dinner with Kelly. I wouldn't want him to acknowledge her in the street. But then I never want my friends to have other friends. I want to be the centre of everyone's attention all the time.'

Harvey laughed. 'Same, actually.'

'It's perfectly healthy,' Cat said, picking up her wine.

'I think it's because of Sam,' Harvey said. 'He was always the centre of attention growing up, you know? And I had to be louder and louder to compete… And then I stopped being loud and just started doing my own thing.'

'Ohhhhh,' Cat said. 'I'm still doing the loud thing. Well, more annoying than loud.'

'You're not annoying,' Harvey said instantly.

Cat laughed. 'Oh, I know I am. Also, people tell me.'

'You're an only child, right?'

Cat nodded. 'That is what I blame it on, yes. But I think it might just be my personality.'

Harvey looked down at his plate – he'd had squid and it was all gone apart from a smear of aioli – and then back at Cat. 'I thought… I would talk to him, um, depending on how tonight goes.'

'Oh!' Cat said, immediately feeling her face heat up. She picked up her wine and took a too large gulp. 'No. I mean. This can't happen. Me and you.'

'Seriously?' Harvey said, pushing a hand back through his hair. When they'd first arrived it had been a little flattened by the hat, but it had recovered its usual swirly-ness.

Cat shook her head. 'I'm sorry if I gave you the impression…'

'No. You didn't. Really. Well. I mean, you did invite me to spend the day with you somewhere clothing-optional…'

'Oh my god.' Cat covered her face with her hands.

'I just… I always had a crush on you.'

Cat shook her head and tried to ignore the fluttering in her belly. 'Fuck off. You didn't.'

'I did. I was never really jealous of Sam – even though everyone thought I was, you know teachers would tell me how great he was at everything, he was on the football team and I'd see how disappointed they were when I fell over my own feet – but I always just thought he was great, you know?'

Cat nodded. She did know. She'd thought he was great too.

'And then he started going out with you and it made me kind of hate him.' He smiled his ridiculous wide smile and Cat smiled back without even thinking about it.

'I didn't think you'd go out with me or anything,' Harvey said. 'And obviously I wasn't going to do anything. Because he's my brother. And then there was that night in the garden…' He shook his head as if trying to clear his thoughts.

'No,' Cat said. She looked around for the waiter. How come her conversations were always being interrupted but when she really wanted one to be there was no one around.

'No?'

'It can't happen. I can't—'

'If I talked to Sam. If Sam was OK with it.'

Cat shook her head again. 'I'm sorry, no. I like you. I always liked you. And I'd like to be friends. I'd love that actually. But we can't be anything more.'

'Ever?'

'Ever.' She stared down at the table for a second and then pushed her chair back, the legs screeching on the wooden floor. 'Just going to pop to the loo.'

In the bathroom, she texted Kelly – *Harvey said he's got a crush on me* – and then peed, washed her hands, and patted some cold water on her face. In the mirror she looked flushed and excited. Her hair had gone a bit flat and weird so she fiddled with it for a while before giving up and hooking it behind her ears. Kelly still hadn't replied, so she took a selfie against the millennial pink tiles and another of her feet on the jade and white patterned tiles and then she saw that Kelly was typing.

Of course he has. You go get some.

I told him I can't.

Why not?!

Cat pressed the call button and as soon as Kelly answered said, 'You know why not.'

'Sam left five years ago,' Kelly observed. 'He's doing stand-up about you. You don't owe him anything.'

'I think I owe it to him to not fuck his brother!' she said, just as the door opened and a short woman with closely cropped red hair looked at her and then looked away again, scurrying into the nearest cubicle.

'Oh god,' Cat said into the phone. 'Now I sound like a sex pest.'

'What if it was just one night,' Kelly said. 'One night to get it out of your system, off your chest, etc. One night and you'll never speak of it again.'

'Something you want to tell me?' Cat asked.

'Got the pregnancy horn but Sean can't get near me without me wanting to chuck. I'm currently enjoying a very healthy fantasy life.'

'So who's your one night.'

'Jason Momoa. I saw a photo of him in a magazine and it made my lady parts beep.'

'I'm going back to my dinner now,' Cat said. 'And will drink until I can no longer remember you just said that.'

'Good luck.'

By the time Cat and Harvey had eaten their mains, they'd finished the bottle of wine and Cat was thinking about what Kelly had said. Not about Jason Momoa, but about the idea of one and done with Harvey. She couldn't really do that though, surely. She'd never been a one-night stand kind of a person and this was Harvey. How would that work? They'd have sex and then just be friends and never refer to it again? She knew people who did do that – a friend had told her that when she'd told a male friend she'd never had an orgasm, he came to her house, went down on her until she did, and then they just went back to being fully dressed, no oral, friends – but Cat didn't see how it would work. But if she took the job in New York. If she was leaving. Then maybe...

What she had seen was the waiter – Charlie – go past with a chocolate mousse that looked pretty good, so maybe she should suggest dessert and take the whole thing one step at a time. Dessert and then maybe coffee and then they'd leave the restaurant and do what? Go on somewhere else? Where she could suggest the one-night thing? And then they could go back to his. For sex. God, she'd drawn a direct line from chocolate mousse to sex; she needed to dial that right back.

'Would you like a look at the dessert menu?' Charlie asked.

Cat looked at Harvey, who was looking back at her with his eyebrows raised. 'Would you like something?'

'Um,' Cat said. 'I thought the chocolate mousse looked—'

'Me too!' Harvey said, beaming. 'Do you want to share one? Or get one each?'

'One each, I think,' Cat said, without actually thinking. Sharing would definitely have been more romantic. But if they were going to do the one-night thing, it wasn't about romance; it would be more like a business transaction. Like at work when a company hired them to fill one specific role rather than contract them for— Jesus, why was she thinking about human fucking resources. She really needed to get laid.

'Wait, no,' she amended, as Charlie turned to walk away. 'I'm not that hungry. I think we can share.'

When she looked at Harvey, he was smiling. She shuffled her chair forward a little, bumping her knee against his under the table. She was giving him mixed messages, she knew, but she could explain when they left the restaurant. She'd suggest they go on somewhere else for another drink and—

'Look!' Harvey said. 'It's snowing.'

CHAPTER TWENTY-ONE

Outside, the snow was still falling, faster than it had appeared from the inside – and it was definitely sticking; the pavement outside the restaurant was already coated white and the park opposite was looking magical.

'I'll walk you to the Tube,' Harvey said. But they hadn't got very far when they realised there was a problem. The street was full of people, the pavements crammed from the kerb to the shop fronts.

'Has something happened?' Harvey asked the nearest person.

'Tube's closed,' a tall man in a turban told them. 'They said temporarily, but it's been bloody ages already.'

'Oh shit,' Cat said. 'See,' she told Harvey. 'I told you! Magical, my arse.'

They walked back the way they'd come and turned onto a side street to cut through and avoid the crowd of disgruntled people.

'We could walk up to Tottenham Court Road,' Harvey said. He took his phone out and tapped at the screen. 'Shit.'

'What?'

'Tube's all fucked up.'

'I told you!' Cat said again.

'It's not the snow,' Harvey said. 'Why would snow affect the Tube anyway, it's underground?'

'My bit's overground,' Cat said.

'There's some sort of massive signal or electrical failure,' Harvey said. 'Fuck, it looks like chaos.'

'I can imagine.'

Harvey put his phone away and looked at her. There were snowflakes on his eyelashes and Cat wanted to brush them off. With her face.

'Do you – this is going to sound bad after our conversation earlier – but you're welcome to stay at mine. I've got a spare bed. Well, a sofa bed. You can have my bed. I changed it this morning. It's really central so as soon as the Tube's sorted, you can, you know, get home no problem.'

Cat thought about the prospect of buses when the Tubes were down. She thought about an Uber but if the traffic was as bad as she suspected it would be, her bank account wouldn't be up to it. Clearly, she didn't have a choice.

'That sounds great,' she said.

Harvey's flat was above an Italian restaurant on the main road.

The entrance hall was dark, but when Harvey flicked on a light nothing happened.

'Shit. Bulb must've gone.'

He tapped the torch on his phone and illuminated the bottom of the stairs.

'I'm only on the second floor.'

Cat followed him, resting her fingers on the wall as she walked.

'I'm not gonna lie,' she said, as they headed up the second flight. 'This is starting to feel a bit murdery.'

Harvey laughed. 'I promise it'll be fine when we get upstairs. We can put all the lights on.'

It was fate. First she'd decided she'd do the one-night thing and then they'd got snowed in and now the lights had gone out. If she'd asked for a sign – she hadn't, but if she had – she'd got three. She rested her fingers on the small of Harvey's back, over his coat, and thought about pushing the coat back off his shoulders and walking her fingers all over him.

He smiled at her over his shoulder – she couldn't really see him, but she could see his smile – and her stomach flipped over. She was really doing this. She was going to Harvey's flat where she would sleep with him. Sam's brother, Harvey. She shouldn't do this. But she was going to. Probably.

Harvey opened the door to his flat and flicked on the lights. A lamp in the far corner of the room, just to the left of an enormous window, and fairy lights strung around a huge photograph of a beach on the wall. Between the two windows there was a small table with a record player and a box of vinyl.

'Wow,' Cat said. 'So who's your friend?' Cat pulled off her boots and put them in the hallway near the front door.

'From drama school,' Harvey said, pulling off his coat and beanie. His cheeks were pink from the cold and his hair was damp at the ends, making it curlier than usual. 'He lives in LA most of the time now, but he likes to keep this place for when he's here.'

'Where do you go when he comes back?'

'Either I sleep on the sofa or I stay with Mum and Dad.' He held out his hand. 'Do you want to give me your coat?'

Cat wriggled out of her coat and handed it over. The back of her neck and the top of her back were wet from the snow and she shivered a little.

'Do you want a shower or something?' Harvey asked, stepping past her to hang the coats up in the tiny entryway.

'No, I don't think so,' Cat said, the thought of being naked in Harvey's apartment giving her butterflies. 'Thanks.'

'A drink then?'

While Harvey was getting wine in the kitchenette, Cat wandered over to look at the photograph on the wall. It was taken from high in the sky, presumably from a helicopter, looking down at the beach. The top half of the photo was bright-blue sea, the bottom half almost-white sand, dotted with multi-coloured sunbathing figures.

'I love this,' Cat said, glancing over at Harvey.

He was heading towards her, holding out a glass, a huge one with just a little wine in the bottom. The first time she'd been given wine like that had been at Kelly's parents' house and she'd been horrified – she'd always previously filled her own wine glasses almost to the top, but she'd got used to it now. Harvey gently tapped his glass against hers and said, 'To snow.'

'To snow,' she said. 'And signal failures.'

She sipped her wine and watched Harvey drink some of his. Then she watched him lick his bottom lip. She wanted to be the one to lick it. What should she say? How did you ask someone to sleep with you once but never again? *That thing we were talking about earlier. You know, when I said nothing could happen? Well, I've changed my mind. Cos you're hot and I'm horny and it probably won't be excruciating.*

She couldn't do it.

Cat woke during the night, desperate for a pee. She sat up and swung her legs off the side of the bed and padded through to the bathroom. The living room door was open – actually she wasn't even sure there was a door – and Harvey hadn't closed the curtains and the snow was still falling, now in great clumps that looked like feathers. The light from a street lamp illuminated half the room and Cat could see Harvey on the sofa bed. He was lying on his back, one arm thrown across his face. One of his long legs was sticking out from under the duvet, bent at the knee. She wanted to bite his inner thigh. Maybe she could've done, if she'd been brave enough to tell him what she wanted. Maybe she could do it now, just go and get in bed with him, whisper it until he woke up.

Instead she tiptoed to the bathroom and peed as quietly as possible, which actually took a fair bit of pelvic floor control, and then scurried back into the bedroom. She pulled the blinds back a little and looked out onto the street. There was a thick carpet of snow now – it was piled on the metal tables outside the cafes and restaurants, gathered on the awnings, topped the streetlights. It didn't look real. There was no one in the street, no traffic, and Cat wasn't sure she'd ever seen London looking so beautiful before.

CHAPTER TWENTY-TWO

'I can't believe I'm doing this again,' Cat said, staring at herself in the mirror in the bathroom of the members' club where Nick's leaving do was taking place.

Her stomach was churning and her palms were sweating. Kelly had had to do her make-up for her earlier because her hands were shaking so much Kelly was scared she'd stab herself in the eye.

'I'm proud of you,' Kelly said.

She was sitting on the chair in the corner now, her swollen legs up on another chair. Cat had told her not to come, since she was still throwing up well past the point of pregnancy that the vomiting was supposed to stop and she wasn't sleeping well either, thanks to heartburn and cramp, but she'd insisted. And since Cat needed the moral support, she'd agreed.

Cat had been nervous that Nick's party would be huge, hundreds of glamorous people she'd feel completely intimidated by, but it wasn't like that at all. She'd walked through the room earlier and it had been warm and friendly. She should have known really. It was very Nick. Even so, the thought of doing stand-up again – and doing it in front of work colleagues who hadn't even known she'd ever done it – was daunting.

'Do you remember the first time we did this?' she asked Kelly.

'I do,' Kelly said. 'I didn't have ankles like an elephant or feel like I was sitting on a bag of grapes.'

'Lovely,' Cat said. 'I was thinking more about how exciting it was.'

'It was,' Kelly said. 'I couldn't believe you were really going to go through with it.'

Cat laughed. She hadn't either. She'd kept telling herself she could back out; she could cancel at any time up until she was actually standing behind the mic. But then she'd been surprised at how comfortable she'd felt there. Her first set hadn't been great, but she'd loved doing it and she'd got a few laughs. Enough to want to try again anyway. Three months later, she'd won a newcomer competition and another three months after that she decided she never wanted to do anything else.

'Have you heard of a meet-cute?' Cat asked, from the small make-shift stage in the corner of the room. 'It's like a funny, story-worthy way to meet someone. Like a "can't wait to tell the grandkids" type of story. A friend of mine met her boyfriend when he was struggling to park his car and she guided him in.' She raised one eyebrow, as a few people laughed. 'Another met a guy on the Tube. She was reading a book, he said he'd read it and it was good; she was excited to meet a man who'd read a book and now they're married.'

There was a light just to her left shining directly in her eye-line and she had to resist the urge to shield her eyes with her hand. She'd get used to it, she knew.

'That was literally the only book he'd ever read, but better than nothing, eh?'

She paused to pick out a couple of faces in the crowd to focus on: Phil from work, who looked significantly more relaxed and about ten years younger than he did in the office, and a woman Cat didn't know with lavender hair and black-rimmed glasses. They were both smiling. Cat smiled back.

'I met my ex when he hit me with his bike,' she said.

She told the story of how she and Sam had met and then told them that he'd worked it into his stand-up routine. Someone actually shouted, 'No!'

'It's true,' she said. 'But it was OK. I did some stuff about him in mine too. We were pretty good at sharing stories. Sometimes if we both wanted the same one, we'd flip for it. He wanted the one about how I accidentally told his mum I was veggie at a barbecue, but I wanted that one cos I thought he'd make me sound like a twat.'

Cat scanned the small crowd until she spotted Kelly. Cat had told her to stay close to the bathroom in case she needed to puke. She should've known she wouldn't listen.

'Anyway,' Cat said, 'we broke up.'

'Good!' someone said in the audience. Cat thought it was probably the same person who'd shouted 'no' but she wasn't sure.

'We broke up five years ago. And then a few months ago, I was on the Tube and the guy opposite was reading the paper – not a book! – and there was my ex. In the paper. The miserable bastard on the Tube wouldn't let me look at his paper. Meet-cute fail. But I got hold of one anyway and it turned out my ex was doing a stand-up routine about me. And our relationship.'

There was actually a gasp of shock at that and Cat laughed. 'I know! I mean, part of me was flattered. Like… why are you so obsessed with me?'

Out of the corner of her eye – the one not currently having the retina burned away by the light – she saw Kelly lurch to her feet.

'Um, that's my best friend Kelly there. Could someone look after her? She's probably about to puke, but she's a pro at it now. You could just hand her a bucket or a bag and she'll be right as rain in a minute.'

She watched as a woman in a very slinky red dress reached for Kelly's arm, guiding her towards the bathroom.

Cat ended with a few words about Nick and how much they'd miss him, how lucky New York was to be getting him, and everyone toasted him.

Nick stepped up on the stage to thank everyone, first hugging Cat and saying 'You are wonderful' in her ear.

'I knew Cat was funny when she asked me out,' Nick told the assembled crowd and got a bigger laugh than Cat had.

Once Nick had given his short speech, he went to the bar to get Cat a drink. Cat popped into the loo to check on Kelly. She was sitting in a chair in the corner, looking pale and wan while the woman in the red dress told her about her business making embroidered sunhats.

'Get back to the party,' Kelly told Cat. 'I'm fine.'

'You don't look fine.'

'I am, promise. Louise is looking after me.' She pointed at the woman in the red dress.

'I'm a big fan,' Louise said. 'Of Kelly's blog, I mean, not of you. Not that I'm not a fan of you. You were good!'

Cat laughed. 'Thank you.'

'Go,' Kelly said.

'Text me if you need me.'

Kelly gave her a thumbs-up, so Cat left.

Nick was just outside the door talking to someone Cat didn't know and she was about to skirt past him when he reached for her arm and handed her a cocktail. His friend drifted away and Nick said, 'Everything sorted for your visit?'

Cat flinched and glanced back at the bathroom door, worried in case Kelly had followed her out, but there was no one else around.

'It's all booked,' Cat said. 'Looking forward to it. How about you? Sorted? Ready?'

Nick nodded. 'I'm just excited to go now. I hate the in-between times, you know? Waiting for something to happen. I just want to get on with it.'

Cat nodded. 'I'm going to miss you around the office though.'

He pulled her into another hug. 'Me too. But not for long, I hope.'

CHAPTER TWENTY-THREE

Cat tiptoed into Arnold's bedroom. It was bigger than her room in her flat and tidier too. She was still sorting out, ready for packing, and she couldn't quite believe she had so much stuff. She told herself she was at the point of organising where things got worse before they got better, but her room was such a disgrace she'd seriously considered just setting fire to the lot.

Kelly had been feeling much better in the days since Nick's leaving party and Sean had convinced her to have a night out – cinema, a meal – so Cat had offered to babysit.

Arnold had shuffled down in his bed so his head was no longer on his pillow and had curled himself around some of his teddies; the soft brown one with the red bow Cat had bought him was closest to his cheek. She gazed at him in the warm glow of a white night light shaped like a bunny, his eyelashes fanned out over his cheeks, his lips pouting out, his chest rising and falling softly with his breath.

Cat loved him so much. She'd loved him from the minute she met him when he was only a few minutes old. She'd been at the hospital with Kelly the entire time, but hadn't stayed for the actual birth, thinking it was a moment for Kelly and Sean alone. Kelly had shouted at her after, said she'd wanted her there, that Sean had been useless (about which Sean had cheerfully agreed, arms wrapped around his wife, beaming with pride).

She didn't know if she could move to New York and leave him. She'd miss him so much. But she'd come back for visits and Kelly and Sean could bring him (and the new baby) over. It would be fun to show Arnold New York: take him to the zoo, on the ferry, up the Empire State Building.

Arnold snuffled in his sleep and Cat leaned down to kiss his forehead. As her lips brushed over his skin, he made an incomprehensible sound and lurched up to sitting, headbutting Cat in the mouth.

'Ow,' Arnold said, sleepily, before falling back down to his pillow again, clutching the teddy to his neck.

Cat had her hand clamped over her mouth, where one of her front teeth was aching and her lip was burning with pain. She waited until she was outside Arnold's door before taking her hand away and muttering, 'MotherFUCKER!' Tasting blood, she tested her lip with her tongue and, yes, it was actually split. She grabbed her front tooth between her thumb and forefinger, expecting it to be loose, but it wasn't, thank god.

In the family bathroom at the end of the landing, she looked at her lip in the mirror, turning it down to better see the injury. There was a clear split, but only a little blood; her lip was already fattening up. Great. She rinsed her mouth with water and headed downstairs. Bloody kids.

When she picked up her phone, she found she had yet another missed call from her dad and she hit the call button before she could change her mind. At least if she spoke to him he'd stop calling for a while and she'd have one less thing to worry about. She really wanted one less thing to worry about.

'Cat!' her dad said. He sounded pleased to hear from her, which surprised her – if she'd been waiting to hear from someone for so long, she'd at least be a little frosty when they finally got in touch, but her dad simply sounded delighted.

'Sorry I haven't got back to you before now,' Cat said.

'Don't worry about that,' her dad said. 'I know how busy you are.'

The thing was, Cat thought, he didn't know how busy she was. Or how anything was in her life. Because she'd never really let him know. She didn't even really know why he wanted to see her. Couldn't they just let the relationship drift away? Wouldn't that make sense? It would surely be easier than whatever they'd been doing all these years.

Guilt curled in Cat's stomach. He was *her dad*. She couldn't just ghost him. She could hear traffic noise in the background and wondered where he was. Maybe he was back home already and they wouldn't have to meet at all.

'So you're in London?' Cat asked.

'Not for much longer actually,' her dad said. 'Off to New York next week. Would be great to see you before I go though.'

Cat's stomach dropped and for a second she couldn't quite catch her breath.

'I'm going to be in New York next week,' she said before she could change her mind.

'No way!' He sounded Australian again. 'Do you think we could get together there instead? Could be fun.'

Strange idea of fun, Cat thought, meeting up with his sullen daughter who'd been avoiding him for months, years. But maybe it was a good idea. Seeing him somewhere neither of them lived. Neutral territory. Less pressure.

'That sounds good,' Cat said. 'I'll text you the dates and where I'm staying and we can sort something out.'

'It's great,' her dad said. 'I'm really glad you called.'

'Yeah,' Cat said. 'Me too.'

When Kelly and Sean came home they were dopey and giggly and affectionate in a way Cat instantly recognised as desperate to go and have sex. Kelly's aversion to Sean must have worn off. She'd have to ask her about it in the morning.

'How was Arnold?' Kelly asked, pulling her coat off and hanging it over the back of a chair.

'Adorable until he headbutted me,' Cat said.

Kelly's face dropped immediately. 'He didn't! What happened?' She stepped out of her shoes and Cat smiled at how much shorter she was.

'It was my own fault,' Cat said. 'I went in to check on him and he just looked so adorable that I tried to give him a little kiss.'

'Oh no,' Sean said from the kitchen.

'I should have warned you about that,' Kelly said. 'It's a recent thing.'

Cat pointed at her lip. 'I'm lucky to still have all my teeth.'

'I just look at him from the door now,' Kelly said. 'Maybe blow him a kiss.'

'I can understand it,' Cat said. 'I wouldn't like someone sneaking up on me while I sleep either.'

'Right?' Kelly said. 'Although it's kind of nice sometimes.'

Sean reappeared with two glasses of water and simply said, 'Yeah?' to his wife.

Kelly's face changed immediately, her cheeks turning pink.

'Too much information,' Cat said.

'We're going to go up, OK?' she told Cat.

'That's fine,' Cat said. 'Leave me here alone. Go and have sex.'

Sean's face flamed, but he was smiling as he turned to leave.

'I know what the glasses are for though,' Cat said, already snuggling back down into the sofa cushions. 'I read that penis beaker thread on Mumsnet.'

'Oh my god,' Sean said as Kelly snorted.

'Please don't remind me of that,' Kelly said. 'You'll ruin the mood.'

'But me getting headbutted in the face didn't,' Cat said. 'Charming.'

'Shut up.' Kelly followed Sean towards the door, calling back 'Love you!' to Cat.

'Love you too,' Cat said, but they'd already gone.

Cat pressed play on the TV to finish watching *The Good Place*. There was no way she was going upstairs until she was confident they were done. She really didn't need to listen to their sex noises; she got enough of that at home. Except it wasn't really home any more. Or it wouldn't be soon.

She ran her finger over her lip as she remembered running her thumbs over Sam's eyebrows back when they were together. Why was she even thinking about Sam? She shouldn't be thinking about Sam. No good ever came of it. But she'd always liked those moments. Sometimes more than the actual sex. The soft moments before or after when they just looked at each other, explored each other's faces with gentle touches. She used to like cupping his jaw in her hand and brushing his chin with her thumb, running her fingers along his cheekbone and the shell of his ear. She missed that a little. Not Sam. Just... that kind of intimacy. Pressing her face into the curve of his neck and knowing exactly what he smelled like right there.

She rolled onto her side and grabbed one of the cushions to pull against her stomach, curling her knees up.

She didn't miss him. Not really. It hadn't been worth it. The pain had been too much. There was no way she was going to put herself through that again. Not with anyone. But sometimes maybe it would be nice just to have someone kiss you gently on the forehead before you fell asleep.

It was just a shame it would always be followed by pain.

CHAPTER TWENTY-FOUR

'This was a terrible idea,' Cat muttered, looking around the foyer of the boutique hotel she and Harvey were reviewing for Kelly. She'd been picturing something huge and over-the-top – she'd actually been picturing the hotel from *Pretty Woman* – but this place was small and modern, all white walls and blond wood and teal and pink accents.

'I dunno, it seems nice,' Harvey said, directly in her ear.

How did he keep sneaking up on her? She turned to smile at him. He'd had his hair cut since she'd last seen him and it was shorter than she'd seen it on him before. It suited him. She wanted to run her fingers along the back of his neck. She bit her thumbnail instead.

'How've you been?' he asked her.

'I'm good,' she said, approaching the reception desk and assuming he'd follow. 'You?'

'Not bad. Thanks.'

They stood smiling at each other and Cat tried to ignore the fluttering in her stomach.

'Does everyone always flirt with you or is it just hotel receptionists?' Cat asked as they walked around the corner to the lift.

Harvey laughed. 'She was just being nice. I don't think you know what flirting is.'

'Oh, I do.' She pressed the down button – their room was a garden room in the basement. 'I've been flirted with. Even done some flirting myself.' She was terrible at it, but she didn't tell him that. 'I know it when I see it.'

'Like porn?' Harvey said, as the lift doors opened and they were faced with an elderly and startled-looking couple.

'What about porn?' Cat asked, against her better judgement, once they were alone in the lift.

'That was a definition in court, wasn't it? The judge said he couldn't define it, but he knew it when he saw it.'

'Oh.' Cat was annoyed to find she was a little disappointed. She hadn't really known what she'd expected and really it was much better for them to stay clear away from any sex-adjacent subjects, but still.

The lift doors opened and Harvey followed Cat to the end of the corridor and their room. Their huge room with doors opening out onto a small, bright, private terrace. Their room with an enormous bathroom containing a giant shower and free-standing bath that was bigger than Cat's entire bathroom. Their room with a flatscreen TV and a squashy sofa and a turntable and collection of vinyl and only one bed.

'There's only one bed,' Cat said. 'I phoned and asked for twin beds. And I sent a follow-up email, and they said—'

'We can change rooms,' Harvey said. 'Want me to ring?'

He'd thrown his weekend bag on the bed and was shrugging his way out of his black coat. Underneath he was wearing a grey hoodie over black jeans.

'It's OK,' Cat said, pulling her eyes away. 'I can do it.'

'Just going for a wee,' Harvey said, unzipping his bag and taking a washbag with him into the bathroom.

Cat rang down to reception and when they told her there were no other rooms free and that there was no way they could swap the beds in the room she had, she texted Kelly a row of the siren emoji. She replied straight away: *What's up?*

THERE'S ONLY ONE BED, Cat sent back.

Jesus, I thought something actually bad had happened. So?

Did you not hear me? I said THERE'S ONLY ONE BED.

So make a pillow wall down the middle if you're that much of a prude or just, you know, don't shag him if you don't want to.

Cat stared at her phone and started typing a couple of times before deleting and trying again. She hadn't yet come up with a reply she was happy with when another one came through from Kelly.

Or is the problem that you DO want to?

'Fucking hell,' Cat said aloud.

Maybe, she typed. *But I can't. So.*

Why can't you?

HE'S SAM'S BROTHER.

So? You and Sam aren't together any more, I'm pretty sure. I remember it happening. I bought you a cake.

Siblings are off limits, everyone knows that.

You literally got that from Friends. You can't let a nineties sitcom run your life.

Sacrilege tbh. But it's def not just Friends. It's a thing. You wouldn't want me shagging your brother, would you?

I haven't got one. But if I did, you'd be welcome to him, I'm sure.

No. It can't happen. And so now I have to share a bed with the sexiest man I've ever met and not lay a finger on him. And I haven't had sex for two years. This is your fault.

This isn't my fault. It's your fault. There's literally nothing to stop you climbing him like a tree.

Cat heard the bathroom door unlock and carried her phone out to the terrace. Harvey always seemed to be sneaking up on her and there was no way she was chancing him reading this conversation over her shoulder.

She hadn't had a chance to reply when another text came through from Kelly.

I've already told you. You should just shag him.

HOW IS THAT HELPFUL? Cat replied.

No-strings sex. How is that not helpful? He might be up for it. And that way you're not really doing the sibling thing. You're just doing the sibling. She followed up with a bunch of laugh/cry emojis and Cat replied, *You're not funny.*

I am. But also I'm serious. Get some. Get some with 'the sexiest man you've ever met'. Get some for me cos I can't stand the way Sean smells so I might never have sex again.

Oh god, Cat replied. *Poor Sean. You seemed into it the other night. When I babysat.*

Thought I was. Turned out I wasn't, Kelly replied. *He's taking it like a champ. As you could be.*

Stop now, Cat typed, laughing as she looked down at her phone. *I need to go and tell Harvey we're top and tailing tonight.*

Kinky, Kelly replied.

'So what are we doing for dinner?' Harvey asked.

He'd taken the news about the bed surprisingly – or perhaps unsurprisingly – well. He'd just shrugged and said it was a big bed and it'd be fine. Then he'd pulled off his hoodie to reveal a plain white T-shirt that rose up as he lifted the hoodie over his head. Cat tried not to stare at the strip of stomach between the waistband of his jeans and the hem of his T-shirt, but she couldn't help spotting the line of dark hair below his navel. And also above. She bit her thumbnail and looked around for the mini bar.

'Want a drink before we go?' she asked.

He dropped his hoodie on the bed and was smoothing his hair back down. It looked soft. Cat wanted to feel it. Drink!

'Do I need to get changed, do you think?' he asked. 'Or will I be OK like this?'

'It's only the hotel restaurant,' Cat said. 'I think you'll be fine.' She pulled open the door of the mini bar. 'Drink?' she repeated.

'I'll have a beer,' Harvey said.

Cat got one for herself too and then flicked the heater on outside, sitting down at the table. The terrace was sheltered with bamboo and some sort of climbing greenery and lit with fairy lights and the glow from the patio heater. It was nice. Cat wished she could relax.

'I know I've said this already,' Harvey said. 'But thanks for inviting me along. Work's been pretty full-on and I don't know when I'll get a chance to get a proper holiday, so these little breaks are good.'

'It's all Kelly,' Cat said. 'Not me.'

'Still.' Harvey smiled at her and then lifted his beer bottle to his lips. Cat looked up at the patio heater. Silver. Red. Hot.

'I appreciate it,' Harvey said and she looked back. Too soon. He was wiping his bottom lip with his thumb and then he licked it, presumably catching a drip of beer.

Cat pinched her own thigh under the table.

'So what's happening with the job?'

While Harvey told her about it – lighting intensities, intelligent fixtures, moving lights, focus position, colour and effects, none of which she really understood – she nodded and smiled and thought about what Kelly had said. Could she just sleep with him? Could she ask him? Just tell him it had been a while and she'd really like to have some sex and if he would too maybe he'd like to have it with her? They had this amazing room and massive bed, it'd be a shame to waste it. And then if it didn't work out, she never had to see him again. They weren't really friends – he was great, but it couldn't go any further, so it was kind of perfect. Wasn't it?

The restaurant was on the top floor of the hotel and entirely glass, overlooking a small outdoor pool with views over London beyond. The sky was almost lavender and streaked with pink clouds.

They ordered wine and then both sat looking out at the view – the sunset reflected in the office building opposite, the Walkie-Talkie building in the distance just beyond.

'How's Arnold?' Harvey asked.

Cat grinned. 'He's great. Not happy about the idea of a new baby, but delightful in every other way.'

'He was cute,' Harvey said. 'When I met him.'

'He liked you,' Cat said. 'Still asks about you.'

They were interrupted by the waitress with the wine. Cat watched in disbelief as she stood too close to Harvey, brushing his arm with her fingers, laughing too loudly, flicking her hair, and ignoring Cat completely.

'Don't even try to tell me you didn't notice that,' Cat asked Harvey once she'd gone.

'What?' he said, his eyes wide, as he picked up his glass and drank some wine, looking at her over the rim.

Cat shook her head. 'It's unbelievable.'

'You just can't tell the difference between politeness and flirting.'

'I really can,' Cat said.

Harvey drank some wine, slowly, still staring at her over his glass, his eyes serious. Cat's breath caught in her chest and she thought again about Kelly's suggestion. What did she actually have to lose? Why couldn't she just have one night? With Harvey. One night of just sex. In a fabulous hotel. With Harvey. No one ever even needed to know. Except Kelly, obviously, she'd tell her everything, but other than her—

'What are you thinking about?' Harvey asked, his voice lower than it had been earlier.

Cat felt her ears heat up. She hoped they weren't actually glowing red against the sunset backdrop.

'What?' she said, brilliantly.

'You had an… interesting expression on your face. I just wondered what you were thinking about.'

'Sam!' Cat blurted out.

Harvey looked briefly startled, jolting back a little in his seat, but he recovered quickly. 'What about him?'

'Just, you know…' Cat looked out through the window at the pool. 'How he's getting on. How the stand-up's going. All that.'

'He's fine,' Harvey said, his voice back at its normal pitch. 'Saw him at Mum's last week for Sunday lunch.'

'And the stand-up?'

'Yeah. It's going well, I think. He'd booked some more shows. He was asking me what you thought of it actually.'

Cat's eyebrows shot up. 'Really? Why doesn't he just ask me?'

'He didn't know if you'd want him to get in touch again. Actually he asked me to ask you if he's OK to friend you on Facebook.'

'Fucking hell,' Cat said. She picked up her wine and drank half the glass. 'Yeah, that's fine,' she said, eventually. 'I can give him some notes.' She picked up her wine again as an excuse not to look at Harvey.

By the time the starters arrived, they'd mostly been talking about Harvey's job again – it seemed a safer subject – but then Harvey asked Cat about hers, and she groaned.

'It's fine. Boring, but fine.'

Cat wondered if she should tell him about the New York offer. Tell him that she was seriously considering it. That it would solve pretty much all of her problems.

'Are you looking for something else?' he asked, lifting a shell off his plate. 'Got any more stand-up planned?'

'What are you doing?' Cat asked him, squinting at his plate. 'What did you order?'

'Oysters,' Harvey said, smirking a little. 'Do you want one?'

'No,' Cat said. 'Thank you.'

She looked down at her own plate. She'd ordered crab with avocado and mango. Distracted by the view and her own spiralling thoughts, she hadn't even heard what Harvey had ordered. Why had he ordered oysters? Was he maybe thinking the same thing Cat had been thinking? Or maybe he just liked oysters.

'I thought since we're not paying…' Harvey said, dipping his head and looking at her from under his eyebrows. He looked like he was up to no good and Cat laughed.

'You make a good point.'

'You really don't want one?' he asked.

Cat looked at his plate and then at his face – he was smiling at her, dimple popping in his cheek – and she said, 'OK then.'

'Have you had one before?' Harvey asked.

'Course,' Cat lied. She watched as Harvey held the shell up to his mouth and tipped the oyster in, swallowed, and then picked up his wine.

As Cat lifted the shell, she remembered an article she'd read about how something like ninety per cent of oysters had norovirus. Which, she remembered now, was why she'd never actually tried one before. Also a news story about a woman who discovered she was allergic to oysters when her very first oyster killed her. Was she really going to eat something that could kill her? Or make her vomit at best? The shell was now resting on her bottom lip, so apparently she actually was. If Harvey hadn't been staring at her – his eyes on her mouth, which was pretty fucking distracting anyway – she'd have thrown it over her shoulder or dropped it down her cleavage. But he was. So she tipped it into her mouth and flicked her head back a little as she tried to swallow it. It was a weird texture. And salty. And it wasn't going down. For a second, Cat panicked that she was actually going to choke on it, but instead her gag reflex kicked in and the oyster launched itself back into her mouth. She grabbed her napkin and managed to get it to her mouth in time to spit it out, her eyes watering.

'Shit!' Harvey said, reaching for the bottle of water on the table and pouring her a glass. 'Are you OK?'

Cat's throat was burning and she didn't trust herself to speak. Instead she nodded and reached for the glass. By the time she'd drunk half of it, her throat felt better and she thought maybe her face had gone back to its normal colour.

'I'm OK,' Cat croaked. 'Shit. Sorry about that.'

'They're not for everyone,' Harvey said. The corner of his mouth quirked.

'Are you laughing at me?' Cat said. 'Cos you know I could've died.'

Harvey did laugh then. 'Died how?'

'I read about a woman who died from an oyster. She was allergic and she just dropped dead.'

'You're not allergic though, right?'

'No.' Cat drank some more wine. 'But I could've choked.'

'But you didn't.' He was still smirking.

'Shut up,' Cat said. She'd finished her wine. Harvey poured more.

'So first it was smoking and now it's oysters. What else are you going to pretend you've done when you haven't?'

That was her chance to say something sexy, Cat thought. Like 'You.' Would that work? Maybe not. But something sexy. Why couldn't she think of anything sexy? Something like… 'Oh there's nothing else I haven't done' with a suggestive eyebrow. Or would that be creepy? Or a bit too Carry On? Harvey was still staring at her, waiting for her answer.

'Oh nothing,' she said. 'Not that I can think of.'

So that was an opportunity missed.

*

They'd both ordered steak for the main and Cat was just cutting into hers when Harvey laughed and said, 'Remember that barbecue? At Mum and Dad's? When you said you were vegetarian?'

'Oh god,' Cat said. 'In my defence, I don't think I actually said I was vegetarian. I think your mum misunderstood and was so bloody lovely she rushed straight out to buy me food.'

'And then wasn't there something else as well?' Harvey said, pausing in cutting his steak to put his head on one side and think.

'No,' Cat lied.

'There was. I'll get it in a minute.' He cut his steak, put it in his mouth, and Cat recognised the exact moment he remembered, because he was smirking again and sped up his chewing in his eagerness to speak.

'You didn't know Pimm's was alcohol!' He grinned.

'Again. A misunderstanding.' Cat stabbed a chip with her fork and looked out past the pool. It was properly dark now – the sky a deep navy – and the pool was lit up turquoise with pink spotlights around the outside and shining up from under the water.

'Doesn't feel like London,' she said, trying to change the subject. 'Feel like I'm on holiday.'

'Where would you go?' Harvey asked. 'If you could go anywhere in the world?'

'I'd like to go to Japan.' Cat picked up her wine glass before realising it was empty again. Harvey topped it up and she drank some before continuing. 'Mostly cos of *Lost in Translation*, you know?'

'I haven't seen it,' Harvey said.

Cat ate a bit of steak, a chip, drank some wine, and said, 'I loved it. You know what it's about, right? Bill Murray and Scarlett Johansson. And they're both alone in this hotel. Well, she's not alone. But she ends up alone. And they hang out and even though I usually hate anything where the man is years older than the woman, they're both so... It's just gorgeous.' She drank some more wine. 'So I've always sort of had this fantasy about being in a hotel and meeting someone randomly and just…' She realised too late what she was saying, where they were.

'Yeah?' Harvey said.

His voice had gone low again. She couldn't even look at him. She looked out at the pool instead but she could see his reflection in the glass, see how he was leaning slightly towards her, his elbows on the table, looking at her intently.

'Um. Yeah. Just, like, a one-off. That no one else would even have to know about. You know?'

She looked at him then and when she saw his expression, her stomach flipped painfully.

'Do you want to—' he started.

'Are we all done here?' The waitress appeared next to Harvey and Cat saw irritation flicker across his face. Good.

'Yes,' Harvey said. 'Thanks. We are, right?' he asked Cat.

Cat had finished her third glass of wine, but the thought of heading back to the room with Harvey was absolutely terrifying.

'I was thinking about another drink maybe? Outside? Is that—'

'That's fine,' the waitress said. 'I'll bring the menu out.'

Harvey pushed back his chair and stood, reaching for Cat's arm. Cat stumbled, bumping her hip against the table. She shouldn't have another drink. Not if she wanted to have sex with him. And she definitely did want to have sex with him. He steered her outside and they stood next to the pool; steam was rising off the surface of the water, the lights turning it pink.

Cat tipped her head back and looked up at the sky. They were in Central London so she couldn't really see any stars, but the moon was bright and clear and she said, 'Look,' before thinking better of it.

'Do you remember that night?' Harvey said.

Cat didn't look at him; she couldn't. She carried on looking at the moon. 'Of course.'

'I always regretted not kissing you,' he said, his voice low again.

The butterflies burst in Cat's stomach again, but they fluttered up her chest and burst out of her mouth as laughter. 'Wait. Earlier. When you were talking in that low voice – like you did just now – was that you flirting?' She looked up at him and he carried on looking up at the moon, but he grinned.

'Yeah. I was trying to demonstrate the difference to you. But I didn't think you got it.'

'I didn't. I thought you were being a bit weird. I didn't know it was flirting.'

'I've got to say,' Harvey said, and then he did look down at her, 'I'm starting to think this flirting thing is a you problem.'

Cat laughed. 'You're probably right.'

They stared at each other. Cat looked at his mouth, the full bottom lip, the scruff of stubble across his jaw. His dimple. She wanted to lick it. All of it.

'I don't think I want another drink,' she said.

'Your poor lip,' Harvey said, frowning at Cat's mouth.

'I know,' Cat said. 'It was very painful.'

Harvey reached up and cradled her jaw in his hand, running his thumb gently across her bottom lip.

Cat stayed very, very still.

'I could kiss it better,' Harvey said, still staring at her mouth.

'I don't think you are magic,' Cat said. Even though she did. 'But you could try.'

Harvey glanced up from her mouth, his eyes crinkling as he smiled.

'I'll be gentle,' he said, his voice slowing.

'I know, I know. I'll just feel a little prick,' Cat said, and immediately regretted it. Why couldn't she just enjoy the moment? Why couldn't she just let Harvey be romantic and sexy and kiss her scabby lip without making stupid jo— oh. Harvey gently brushed his lips across hers and she lost her train of thought entirely. His hand was still on her face, fingers pressing gently behind her ear. He brushed her lip with his thumb again before another gentle lip-brush and then followed it with his tongue.

Cat heard herself make an embarrassing sound. At some point, her eyes had closed, so she opened them again and looked at Harvey's eyelashes, at the little line between his eyebrows. He was concentrating. Concentrating on kissing Cat. She closed her eyes again.

His thumb dipped between her lips, brushing against her tongue and Cat had to fight every instinct to either pull back and run away or push him down on his back and kiss him unconscious.

'Better,' Harvey murmured.

'Huh?' Cat blinked her eyes open.

'Your lip,' Harvey said, smiling slowly. 'Is that better.'

'Um.' Cat swallowed. 'No. I think I need more… treatment.'

God. This was turning into bad role play. Next thing she'd be offering to dress up as a sexy nurse and asking him to tie her up with a stethoscope.

Harvey laughed. 'That's what I thought.'

And then he kissed her again. This time it wasn't a gentle brush of lips, he kissed her like he'd been thinking about kissing her forever, like he couldn't wait and never wanted to stop. Cat wrapped her arms around his neck and pulled him closer.

CHAPTER TWENTY-FIVE

Cat pushed the key card into the slot and it flashed red.

'Fuck OFF,' she muttered, pulling it out and trying again. Red again. She could feel Harvey close behind her. He wasn't touching her, but heat seemed to be emanating from his body or maybe it was his aura or some shit. Whatever it was, he was right there and she couldn't seem to get the fucking door open.

She pushed the card in again, wiggled it a little and held her breath, but no, red again.

Harvey reached around her and took the card out of her hand.

'I think it's upside down.' His voice was right next to her ear and her knees went weak. He flipped the card over, pushed it into the slot and the indicator glowed green.

'Thank fuck,' Cat breathed, pushing open the door.

Once they were inside the room, Cat pushed Harvey back against the door and pressed up against him, dipping her head against his chest. She took a deep breath. They were really going to do this. She was really going to sleep with Harvey. Just once. So they'd better make it count.

She slid her hands over his hips and up under the hem of his T-shirt. His skin was soft and warm and she pressed her fingertips against his flesh. He wasn't moving and he seemed to be holding his breath. She looked up to find him looking down at her, his bottom lip captured between his teeth and a look of what seemed to be awe on his face.

'What the fuck,' she whispered. 'Harvey.'

'I've thought about this so much,' he said. 'Since that night. In the garden. Since before that night, if I'm honest. I can't believe it's actually happening.'

'Jesus,' Cat said. She stretched up on tiptoes to touch her lips to his. They were warm and soft too and he gasped against her mouth. Almost immediately she was overwhelmed with him. Kissing wasn't going to be enough. She wanted him naked on the bed. She wanted to crawl all over him. Instead she hooked one hand around his neck and pulled him down to meet her mouth again. He pushed his hands into her hair and guided her head to one side, deepening the kiss, before pulling away and tracing his lips over her neck.

'God,' she murmured, letting her head drop back. She pressed up against him, pushing him back against to door, his thigh between both of her legs. She slid her hands up under his shirt, fingers gliding over his ribs, knuckles grazing the hair on his chest until she was holding onto his shoulders under his shirt. She could feel the muscles moving as he wrapped one arm around her and used it to hold her more firmly against his chest. She hooked one leg up over his hip, half-hoping he might lift her up, and carry her over to the bed. She wasn't sure if she could walk.

'It's been a while,' she said against his neck, kissing down the cord of muscle towards his shoulder.

'Yeah?' he murmured, fingers pressing into the nape of her neck, tongue drifting across her lower lip.

'Yeah. Can we…' She used the door to push herself backwards, away from him, creating a little space between them for the first time since they'd got back to the room.

Harvey didn't move, waiting for her to direct him. It was hot as hell.

'Bed,' she said.

*

Harvey was asleep. Afterwards, he'd stayed awake long enough to hold her and kiss her and tell her how amazing she was and how great it had been, but he'd started to doze as he was talking and then he'd snuggled into her side and drifted off.

Cat had been staring up at the ceiling for at least an hour. She'd wriggled out from under Harvey's arm and found her phone in the pocket of her jeans, but it was too late to text Kelly. There was a possibility that she was up puking (or eating gross yellow food), but it was more likely that she was asleep and had forgotten to turn her notifications off and Cat couldn't risk waking her up. Instead she'd gone for a pee, got a bottle of water out of the minibar, taken her make-up off, cleaned her teeth and stared at herself in the mirror until her eyes had blurred. And now she was back in bed.

Harvey was snoring gently, his mouth hanging open. Cat wanted to kiss him. His mouth and his eyebrows and his cheekbones and his jaw. His neck and shoulders and arms and ribs. She wanted to bite his nipple and trace her tongue along the line of hair that ran almost from his throat to his crotch. She'd done all of that already, but she really really wanted to do it all again. Instead, she lay on her back and stared up at the ceiling.

It wasn't like the ceiling at home, with cracks and cobwebs and a brown water stain in one corner; it was smooth and clean and pristine, and Cat could see all the mistakes she'd made in her life scrolling across it as if it were a cinema screen.

She'd already watched her childhood and most of her teens. She'd watched her dad leaving and her mum falling apart. And she knew what was next so she rolled onto her side and tried to sleep, but she was kidding herself. Even with eyes closed, without the blank page of the white ceiling, she could still see how she and her mum struggled after her dad left. How her mum worked various jobs to fit around Cat and school. How she'd cleaned for friends who'd treated her like shit, and then for companies who treated her like shit. How Cat had taken shitty weekend jobs to help out but there was still never enough. And how then she'd moved to London and left her mum alone. Her mum had said she would be fine, was fine, had insisted that Cat go, said she wanted better for her than she had. Even said that Cat's dad was going to help out, but Cat was pretty sure he never had. And then her mum hadn't even told her when she'd got her breast cancer diagnosis; Cat had found out from one of her mum's friends, who had no idea she didn't know. And Cat had managed to bluff her way through the rest of the conversation, her chest hurting and throat burning, desperate to get away so she could phone her mum.

She'd gone home that weekend and her mum told her that originally she hadn't wanted to worry her and she'd thought it would all be dealt with quickly. But it had spread and the prognosis wasn't good. Cat had gone home to look after her mum, but she'd died just a few weeks later.

'Hey,' Harvey said.

Cat looked over. He was still in the same position – on his side, face smushed into the pillow – but she could see his eyes glittering in the dark.

'Hey,' she said back, rolling onto her side to face him.

'Sorry I fell asleep,' he said.

'That's OK. You exerted a lot of energy.'

He grinned. 'You too. But you're still awake.'

'I started thinking,' Cat said.

'Oh no.'

'I know, right? I usually try to avoid it, but sometimes...'

'Is there anything I can do to distract you?' He reached out and rested his hand on her hip and she shivered even though the room was perfectly warm.

'No, it's OK. You can sleep.'

'Listen, if we've only got one night, I don't want to waste it sleeping.'

He was shuffling closer, his hand curled around her waist now.

'Oh, I told you that, did I? I obviously had more wine than I thought.'

'You had three glasses. But yeah. You told me. Like *Lost in Translation*, right? One and done.'

'They didn't actuall—'

But she didn't get to finish because Harvey kissed her. And she let him roll her on top of him and brace his hips with her thighs. And then she stopped thinking about her mum and university and everything that was wrong with her life. And she thought about Harvey instead.

CHAPTER TWENTY-SIX

'I can't believe you actually did it,' Kelly said, glancing over at the garden where Sean and Arnold were working on a snowman.

She was leaning back on the sofa, propped up against a pile of cushions, a bowl of frozen peas balanced on her growing belly. Occasionally she grabbed it when she felt a kick and pointed it out to Cat, but Cat hadn't caught one yet.

'Me neither.' Cat grinned. She was eating a family bag of Giant Chocolate Buttons.

'It was obviously good. Since you can't stop smiling.'

'It was really good. I mean, that's not right. Good isn't a strong enough word. It was amazing. The best—'

'Ah.'

'What?'

'I mean, I wasn't going to ask.'

'It's awful though, isn't it?' Cat curled her hands around her mug of tea. 'To compare them, I mean. But how could I not?'

'Did you talk to Harvey about it?'

'About him being a better shag than his brother? Yeah, I printed him a certificate.'

'Not that! About the whole… situation.'

'No. I mean, not last night. We did the first time we had dinner. After the spa.'

'And?'

'I told you. We agreed not to talk about him.'

'So you're both pretending this isn't anything.'

'We're not pretending. It isn't anything. It's no-strings sex.' Cat sipped her drink. 'It was your idea!'

'Tell me about it,' Kelly said, glancing at the garden again. 'Give me all the sordid details.'

Cat laughed. 'No! Don't be weird.'

'Did you go on top? Did he go down on you? Did you go down on him? What's his dick like?'

'Your child is right there!' Cat said, pointing to Arnold in the garden.

'He's busy, he's not listening. Come on, tell me. I'm really horny.'

'So have sex with your super-hot husband. Look at him!'

They both looked out at the garden where Sean was patting an enormous sphere of snow while Arnold hopped up and down with excitement.

'He is super hot, isn't he,' Kelly said. 'Pregnancy hormones are such a bastard. I already miss his parts.'

'Should I go and tell him to get them out? I'll finish the snowman off, Sean can finish you off.'

'Don't tempt me.'

She pushed her bare toes into the side of Cat's thigh. 'So when are you seeing him again?'

'I told you,' Cat said, sandwiching two Buttons together. 'We're not. It was just the one night. We agreed.'

'But you want to see him again.'

Cat sighed and stacked four Buttons together in a little tower. 'I mean, if literally everything was different, yeah. But it's not. So.'

The problem was Cat couldn't stop thinking about Harvey. Since they'd slept together, he was on her mind all the time. She woke up thinking about him. She went to sleep thinking about him. When she didn't have any work to do, she scrolled deep into his Facebook. She even dreamt about him. It was becoming a problem.

'Just. Fucking. Call. Him,' Kelly said when Cat went over after work.

Kelly wasn't throwing up quite as much but she felt like she was going to almost all of the time. Sean was working shortened hours and Kelly was spending every minute he was home lying in a darkened room. Cat lay across the foot of her friend's bed and idly massaged her feet.

'No,' Cat said. 'I've told you. We're done. I cut it off.'

'Brutal.' Kelly smiled. 'What if you took him to New York?'

Cat had finally told Kelly that she was going out to New York for work, but not that Nick had offered her a job out there. For a second, Cat considered Kelly's suggestion – New York with Harvey would be amazing. They'd have fun. In and out of bed. If they ever actually made it out of bed.

'No, that would be way too distracting.'

'God, yeah.' Kelly rolled her eyes. 'All that distracting sex. Terrible. Just tell me why you won't even consider actually trying to make this work,' Kelly said.

'I've told you why.'

'Because you think you'll hurt him. Or you think you'll get hurt.'

'Because I've been here before and it doesn't work out. And Harvey's so... I couldn't bear it when it inevitably ended.'

Kelly groaned and Cat wasn't sure if it was because of the pregnancy or the conversation.

'But what if it didn't end? What if you fell madly in love and lived happily ever after?'

'We wouldn't.'

'If it didn't work out that would be bad, yeah. But if you don't even try—'

'I've tried. With Sam. Before Sam. Everyone leaves.'

'That's not true,' Kelly said.

But it was. Cat knew it was. She could give Kelly plenty of examples. But when she'd finished massaging her feet, Kelly was asleep.

CHAPTER TWENTY-SEVEN

Cat had read an article about how airports are liminal spaces. Places you'd never go unless you were going – or coming back from – somewhere else. So they sort of exist outside of normal life. Like limbo.

Cat's life felt like limbo at the moment. Had for a while, in fact. (Possibly for five years, but she didn't really want to accept that.) The trip to New York, the idea of moving to New York, was the first step in changing this. Which was why, she assumed, her stomach had been churning with nerves since the moment her alarm had gone off that morning.

But now she was in New York, putting the key in the door of the Airbnb Nick had arranged for her – better than a hotel for giving her an idea of what living there would be like, he'd said – and the nerves were starting to switch to excitement.

The apartment was beautiful – small, but bright and funky with a spiral staircase up to the bedroom and a balcony looking out over the rooftops and into other people's windows. In the morning, she pulled her boots and coat on over her pyjamas and walked to the nearby bodega for a coffee and a pastry, before taking them out on the balcony to watch New York wake up.

She spent her first day on a bus tour, hopping off and wandering anywhere that looked interesting. Nick took her for dinner at a stupidly expensive (seven dollars for sautéed onions) steak restaurant and gave her the hard sell on New York. She didn't tell him that she'd all but made her mind up.

By the second morning the old Italian brothers who ran the bodega around the corner greeted her like family, the taller one teasing her about her accent and the fact that she was in her pyjamas; the smaller, rounder one telling him to be nice and patting Cat's cheek with his wrinkled hand.

RMJ's New York offices were a couple of minutes' walk from Penn Station. They weren't much bigger than the London offices, but they were more modern, with glass partitions, access to a roof terrace and, of course, views over Manhattan. Nick showed her around, introducing her to everyone, and took her into what would be her office. It was small and plain but it had a window and it was an office. Just for her. In New York.

From there, Nick took her downstairs for burgers and beers at a roof bar next to Madison Square Garden.

'So?' he said, as Cat was taking her burger apart because there was no way she'd fit it in her mouth otherwise. 'What do you think?

Cat took a bite of her burger to postpone having to answer.

'Good, right?' Nick said.

Cat nodded, her mouth full. When she'd finished chewing, Nick was still staring at her, waiting.

'It's all amazing,' she said. 'This whole visit. The offices. The fact that you even thought of me at all.'

'This sounds like it's going to be a no,' Nick said. 'Let me try to convince you.'

'It's not a no,' Cat said. 'But it's not a yes either. Not yet. Is that OK?'

'Take all the time you need.' Nick picked up his own burger. 'I mean, I need to know within the next couple of weeks.'

Cat laughed. 'Right.'

'No pressure.' Nick grinned at her from behind his bun.

CHAPTER TWENTY-EIGHT

Cat sat in the window of the Upper West Side Starbucks her dad had suggested they meet in because it was easy to find. Cat could have got an Uber there, but instead she'd walked from the apartment, zigzagging between the avenues and cross streets to get an overview of bits of the city she wouldn't normally have a chance to see.

She'd expected it to be freezing, colder than it was at home, but it was unseasonably warm for February – the sun bright and the air brisk, perfect walking weather. She'd stopped at a corner bodega for a bottle of water, paying with a handful of change she peered at but still couldn't quite work out. The woman serving had picked the correct coins out of Cat's hand and she'd felt like a total loser. But honestly, the coins all looked the same.

She was half an hour early, so she nursed her latte and people-watched out of the window. The traffic – both vehicle and pedestrian – was constant. Tiny elderly ladies hunched over their Zabar's bags. Groups of tourists chattering excitedly. A crocodile of children in matching T-shirts, tiny backpacks over their shoulders. They made Cat miss Arnold. She took a photo through the window and sent it to Kelly.

As entertaining as the view was, Cat jumped every time the door opened. At eleven – the time they'd arranged to meet – she considered moving so it was directly in her field of vision, but she decided it was too desperate. She got herself another drink – fizzy water; she didn't think any more caffeine would be sensible – and returned to her window stool, her phone on the ledge in front of her in case her dad texted that he was running late. Or something.

At eleven-thirty, Cat bought a burnt chocolate brownie and returned to her post at the window and texted Kelly to say she didn't think he was coming.

He will, Kelly replied. *He's probably running late. Hang on. Love you.*

The 'love you' made Cat think Kelly wasn't entirely convinced he was going to turn up and she was almost certainly right. Cat bit a corner of the brownie and berated herself for falling for it again. Her dad had let her down so many times but every single time he turned up she expected him to have changed. Why? He'd never change. He never would. People don't.

The door opened and Cat turned. It was a short stocky man in overalls. Cat licked her finger and gathered some brownie crumbs from the plate. But why? Why ask to see her? Why get her hopes up if he had no intention of turning up? It made no sense. Unless he just wanted to torment her and why would he do that? Although he'd tormented her mum enough; maybe he missed it since she'd died.

Cat finished the brownie and texted Kelly again. *He's not coming.*

Have you texted him? Kelly replied.

Cat sighed. Yeah. That would be the practical thing to do, she knew. But she didn't want to text. Didn't want to get the reply saying he'd forgotten or something had come up or some other bollocks. At least she still had hope. A little. Maybe.

I'll text at 12, Cat replied. And then checked the time. He had five minutes. Or she did. Five minutes of hope left. She finished her water and tried to tell herself to enjoy being in New York. She was in New York! For business! Like an adult! She wouldn't let her dad ruin it, like he'd ruined so many other things.

She watched the time on her phone flick over to 12:00 and thumbed it open.

Hey, she typed. *Where are you?*

After five minutes, she got herself another coffee and texted Kelly again. *No reply.*

I'm sorry, love.

And then: *Are you sure you're in the right Starbucks?*

Cat rolled her eyes at her phone. Of course she was in the right fucking Starbucks, she wasn't a complete idiot. She opened the text her dad had sent her and swivelled on her stool until she spotted a barista refilling the packaged coffee stand.

'Excuse me,' she said, sounding extremely English to her own ears. 'Is there another Starbucks near here?'

The woman rolled her eyes and then smiled to soften it. 'I think there's, like, twenty?'

'But not on Broadway?' Cat said, already starting to feel panic creeping up her spine. But, no. Her dad would have texted her. Why wouldn't he have texted her?

'Oh no,' the barista said, laughing. 'There's... how many branches do we have on Broadway?' she called to her colleague behind the counter, an enormous blond man who Cat had noted looked like a Viking.

'I think nineteen,' the Viking called back without looking back from the coffee machine.

'That's on the whole of Broadway,' Cat's barista told her. 'Did you have a cross street?'

Cat double-checked her phone again – still no new text. 'Yeah, Eighty-first.'

'This is Seventy-fifth,' the barista said.

Cat's stomach lurched and the palms of her hands prickled. 'It can't be.'

The barista smiled sympathetically. 'You need to walk up about five blocks.' She pointed out of the window back the way

Cat had originally come. 'Look for Zabar's on your left and it's just after.'

'Great,' Cat said. 'Thank you.' She grabbed her coffee and bag and slid off her stool. She was an idiot. A complete idiot.

As she walked, she wondered how she could possibly have fucked it up. She'd planned her zigzag journey on the map before setting off. She'd checked the cross streets as she'd walked, she was sure. How had she gone five streets beyond where she meant to end up? And why hadn't she checked the address when she arrived? She knew why, she remembered; it was partly because her hands had been frozen and she'd been dying to wrap them around a hot cup of coffee, and partly because she'd been impressed that there'd been a Starbucks exactly where she'd expected there to be one when she'd planned her route. She'd somehow forgotten that a Starbucks on a corner was hardly the fucking One Ring.

She crossed 76th Street, narrowly avoiding a woman in short shorts on a motorised scooter, enormous headphones covering her ears, and carried on past a CVS and a Marshalls, both of which Kelly had told her she should visit, but she hadn't yet. She crossed 79th, glancing over at a church on the opposite corner that looked like a Disney castle. And then there was Zabar's and then the correct Starbucks.

'There's no way he'll still be here,' she muttered to herself as she pushed the door open, butterflies swirling in her belly.

She was right.

He wasn't.

Cat was in the wine bar opposite the apartment when her phone buzzed with a text from her dad. She took a gulp of her second glass of ridiculously expensive red (seriously, they were charging double for a glass what Cat paid for a bottle at home, and that was if she was buying a decent bottle) before tapping it open.

Sorry my phone was off earlier, he'd texted. *Forgot the plugs are different here.*

Cat took another gulp of wine and stared out across the dark street. The front of the wine bar was open to the sidewalk and while 84th Street was quiet with just the occasional dog walker wandering past; she could look over at Columbus Avenue, still busy with trucks and yellow cabs, a Coca-Cola van making a delivery to the deli on the corner.

She'd texted her dad from the second Starbucks to tell him what had happened, how she'd fucked up. She'd half expected him to say he'd come back (assuming he'd been there in the first place) but once again he hadn't replied. She'd bought another coffee (that had definitely been a mistake, she'd been jittery as fuck all afternoon) and waited another hour in case he popped back to check. But no. Nothing.

Cat had got an Uber back to the apartment, texting with Kelly the entire way. Kelly had assured her that it was a mistake anyone could have made and not to beat herself up about it. But Cat was furious with herself anyway. And also, unreasonably, furious with her dad for putting her in a situation where she ended up feeling like shit. Even though it was her own fault she felt like shit.

She'd dragged herself up the six flights of stairs to the apartment and spent a couple of hours in the bath, listening to increasingly morose music, before heading out to the incredibly expensive wine bar.

'I should eat something,' she said to herself aloud. The waiter brought a menu almost instantly and Cat ordered a plate of cheese and charcuterie, along with a third glass of wine. She texted her dad to tell him she wouldn't have time to see him now, something had come up with work. And then she texted Nick and told him she'd take the job.

CHAPTER TWENTY-NINE

Back in London, Cat was determined to sort everything out as quickly as possible. She took a couple of days off work and dedicated them to clearing her room, filling three bin bags with rubbish, taking two more to the charity shop and boxing everything else up. She didn't know what she was going to take to New York with her, thought she'd probably have to put some stuff in storage and decide at a later date, but for now her room was clear and clean and she could relax.

Colin had been sweet about the New York job, telling her there would always be a job for her in London if she changed her mind.

'I won't change my mind,' Cat had said. And then she'd spent a few days making sure her entire caseload was up to date.

Once her room was sorted, she dedicated her evenings to researching New York – what she needed to do before she got there, tips on relocating – and let herself feel excited, even though she woke up every morning feeling like there was a boulder on her chest. And the boulder was the idea of telling Kelly. And Harvey.

Harvey had texted a few times – cute, flirty messages that made Cat's heart vibrate in her chest. She'd replied in what she thought was a friendly tone, but she actually wondered if maybe they couldn't get together one more time before she left. Plus Georgie and Pete were painting the living room and it would be a relief to get away from the fumes.

Are you free tonight? she texted Harvey.

Yep. Want to go out?

Thought I could come to you.

He replied with five smiley emojis and Cat laughed. What a dork.

'God, you're freezing,' Harvey said, as soon as Cat was through his door. Even so, he started to push off her coat and she wriggled out of it, pressing up against him, rubbing her face into his neck, even though she'd told herself the entire way there she wouldn't. He smelled so good. He always smelled so good.

His hands were under her top already, palms sliding over her ribs.

'Yeah?' he said, his mouth right next to her ear.

'Yeah. Please. Just—'

'Just once, I know,' Harvey said.

This once would make it twice, but Cat wasn't going to think about that. It would be the last time and that was the main thing.

His skin was warm and hers was freezing. She wanted to climb inside him. He lifted her top over her head and it caught on her earring. She flailed a little from inside the fabric until she managed to free herself, and the way he was looking at her made her want to cry.

She was moving to New York. She was starting again. This was the last time she'd get to have him. She shivered.

'Shit, you're so cold,' Harvey said, dipping his head to kiss the side of her neck. 'Do you want to get in the shower?'

'Fuck,' Cat said. 'Yes.'

She followed Harvey into the bathroom, tugging at his jumper as he undid his jeans and pushed them down, yanking off his socks and turning back to undo Cat's jeans because her fingers were too cold to free the button. She sat on the edge of the bath to take her own damp socks off and when Harvey reached past her to turn the shower on, she bit the inside of his arm.

What if she could get him to come to New York with her? There were loads of theatres in New York, she was sure he could find work there. And they could start again together and no one would even need to know. The water thundered down behind her – rich people always seemed to have great water pressure – and Cat pulled her bra off over her head and pushed her knickers down to fall on the tile floor.

'Careful,' Harvey said, when she climbed into the shower after him. 'Slippy.'

Her chest hurt. She tried to breathe slowly, inhaling the steam from the hot water, crown of her head on Harvey's chest, her hands curled around his hips.

He looked really good wet. Even better than usual. He should be wet all the time. She pressed him back against the tiles and he winced at the cold. She kissed his neck, his shoulders, his arms. She turned around and let him slide his hands over her body, his mouth on the back of her neck. He washed her hair, his fingers gentle on her scalp and it made her shiver. No one had ever washed her hair before. She didn't think she'd like it. She liked it. She turned in his arms and hooked one leg up against his hip, pressing their bodies together until Harvey tipped his head back, groaning, and she licked the water off his throat, his hand sliding down between her legs, fingers probing gently.

She tipped her head back so the water ran over her face and neither of them could tell she was crying.

'Cat,' Harvey said later, in the dark. She hadn't intended to stay. She'd stayed anyway.

'What?' She'd reached his ribs now and tried running her tongue along one. Harvey squirmed away from her.

'Why don't we tell Sam? I'm serious.'

Cat leaned up on her elbows and stared at him. At his perfect eyebrows and straight nose and full lips. He was too pretty. It was ridiculous.

'I can't,' she said. Hurt flickered across Harvey's face and Cat felt her chest tighten. She dropped her head and mouthed along his shoulder.

'Why not?'

Cat took a shuddery breath and shuffled up the bed, leaning back against the pillows. 'I need to tell you something.'

Harvey rolled onto his side to look up at her.

'I'm moving to New York. That's what I was over there for last week. I've had a job offer and I've taken it and I'm moving.'

Harvey rolled onto his other side and sat up on the edge of the bed. Cat stared at his wide back and then said, 'Say something.'

'What is there to say?' he asked, looking back at her over his shoulder. 'I think you need to leave.'

It was the right decision, Cat told herself on the Tube home. She knew it was. Nothing could happen between them. Nothing more than already had. And she'd told him it was a one-off. He'd known that. Yes, she'd come back again tonight, but she'd made it clear. It wasn't fair for him to expect more from her.

It was for the best anyway. They never would have worked.

CHAPTER THIRTY

Cat was woken by her phone ringing repeatedly and she almost fell out of bed trying to get to it. The screen said Kelly, but when Cat answered, it was Sean.

'Kel's in labour,' he said. 'Can you come?'

Cat pulled her boots and coat on over her pyjamas and ran straight out of the house.

'Is she OK?' Cat said when she finally found Sean at the hospital. She'd grabbed a taxi from home and spent the journey alternately worrying about Kelly and trying not to picture the hurt on Harvey's face when she'd told him she was leaving.

Sean looked exhausted. To a stranger, he probably still looked perfect – groomed and smart and together – but Cat knew him well enough to see the tension in the set of his shoulders and jaw, the lines pulling at the corners of his eyes.

'She's good,' he said, smiling weakly. 'She's so amazing. I'm pathetic.'

'You're not pathetic!' Cat said, dropping into the seat next to him and bumping him with her shoulder.

He shook his head. 'I want to be able to help, you know?'

'But how can you? She's pushing a person out of her chuff. You made your contribution months ago, it's all on Kel now.'

'I know,' Sean said. 'But I read the books, you know? I made a playlist and brought snacks and camomile tea and a... TENS machine? She doesn't want any of it. She told me to go away.'

'Did she say "go away"?' Cat asked, smiling.

'Piss off,' Sean muttered.

Cat laughed. 'I've read the books too, you know.' Well, she'd looked at a couple of websites. 'This is normal. You did everything you could. But neither of you could know what she'd want or how she'd feel when it actually happened. It was the same with Arnold, right?'

Sean nodded, slumping back in the uncomfortable moulded plastic chair and rubbing his face with both hands.

'And now you're out here giving me a pep talk when she wants you in there.'

'Jesus,' Cat said. 'You're right. Should've just left you out here crying.' She bumped him with her shoulder.

'I wasn't crying,' he said. And he sounded so much like Arnold that Cat wanted to sniff him and tell him he smelled like patriarchy and Tom Ford cologne. Instead she wrapped one arm around him, squeezed hard, and said, 'Shall we go in?'

Cat stopped so suddenly in the doorway that Sean bumped into the back of her.

'Sorry,' she muttered, but she was staring at Kelly.

'Is that Cat?' she heard Kelly say from under a hanging curtain of hair.

Cat crossed the room and stopped next to the chair Kelly was kneeling on, the wrong way round.

'Hey,' Cat said, her throat tight.

'Glad you're here.' Kelly rested her cheek against the back of the chair and looked up at Cat. Her face was pale and slick with sweat.

'The fuck are you doing, Kel?' Cat asked.

Kelly was up on her knees, leaning over the back of a pale-blue plastic padded chair. There was a monitor stuck to her back, more wires emerging from beneath her green hospital gown.

'It's easier this way,' Kelly panted, shifting and turning slightly towards Cat. 'I tried on my back, but it was fucking horrible. And then I got in the pool, but I threw up.'

'Lovely,' Cat said. 'I brought your husband back with me. You should be nicer to him; he's doing his best.'

'Oh god,' Kelly said. 'Shut up. He got me in this predicament. Babe,' she said to Sean, who appeared almost instantly at her other side and started rubbing gently between her shoulders.

Cat's eyes welled up instantly. 'You guys.'

'You're not allowed to be in here if you're crying,' Kelly said. 'That's why I chucked Sean out before.'

Cat laughed. 'You didn't tell me that!'

Sean looked slightly shamefaced. 'She's just so amazing, I can't—'

'I know,' Cat said, looking down at Kelly, who was pressing her face against the back of the chair, eyes screwed up.

'I swear to god,' Kelly said through gritted teeth. 'If you don't shut up I'll make them throw you out of the hospital, never mind the room.'

Cat laughed. 'God, you're obnoxious when you're pushing a person out of your fanny. What can I do that you won't shout at me for?'

'There's a hairband in my bag, but Sean can't find it.'

'I don't think it's in there, babe,' Sean said, his voice small.

'It is,' Kelly said. 'It definitely is.'

'OK.' Cat picked up the fancy leather hospital/baby bag she knew Kelly had been sent by a PR and undid the main zip.

'I think it's in a side pocket,' Kelly said.

'You didn't tell me that!' Sean said.

'I did, babe.'

Cat opened all the pockets and rummaged through baby wipes, tissues, sanitary towels, nail files, a neck pillow and two packets of Tangfastics.

Until she found the hair tie, wrapped around a lip balm.

'Got it,' she said, smoothing Kelly's hair back from her face and fastening it into a low ponytail.

'Oh, thank fuck,' Kelly moaned. She turned to Sean. 'I told you.'

He dipped his head to kiss her forehead. 'Sorry, baby.'

Cat turned away and redid all the zips on the bag, her stomach clenching painfully.

'Oh fuck,' Kelly said, her voice low. 'I can... I think this...'

She curled over, pressing her head into the back of the chair and groaning. Cat met Sean's eyes, wide and scared. They both watched Kelly as she went rigid, one arm flailing in Sean's direction. He took her hand and she gritted out, 'No!', so he let it go again and rested it on the back of her neck.

'Fuck!' she said, moments later when her entire body seemed to have relaxed. 'That hurt like—'

'How are we getting on?'

Kelly rolled her eyes so dramatically that Cat laughed out loud. Sean moved around the chair to stand next to Cat and the midwife started checking the various monitors.

'You're doing very well,' she told Kelly.

'I just had a really strong contraction,' Kelly said.

The midwife glanced at her and back at the monitor. 'Oh, that was just a little one. They'll get much worse than that.'

'Why the fu—' Cat started to say, but Sean touched the back of her hand with his.

'Thanks,' Kelly said. 'That's helpful.'

'Good to be prepared, I always say,' the midwife said. She stopped fiddling and turned to look at Cat and Sean.

'You two look useless. Anything they could be doing, Mum?'

Kelly closed her eyes. 'No. We're good. Thanks.'

'I'll come back in a bit and check on you then.' She was already halfway out of the room.

'Don't hurry,' Kelly said, as the door swung closed behind her.

'Jesus,' Cat said.

'I know. Amazing bedside manner,' Kelly said.

'Is there really nothing we can do?' Cat asked her.

'You could try the TENS machine again.'

'I thought you didn't—' Sean started.

'Babe,' Kelly said. 'You were pressing it at the wrong time and electrocuting me. And then you missed the bit when the contraction actually peaked. Cat might have a bit more co-ordination.'

'I might not,' Cat said. 'But what's a bit of light electrocution between friends?'

'Sorry,' Sean said. 'I—'

'Stop apologising,' Kelly said, tipping her face up to look at him. 'Come and kiss me.'

'Seriously?' Sean said, his cheeks turning pink.

'Just a kiss, babe,' Kelly said. 'I'm not asking you to do me over the monitor.'

Cat snorted with laughter and picked up the TENS machine, which seemed to be a small box, trailing wires with sticky pads on the ends.

'Do I just stick—' Cat started, but when she looked up, she found Sean was now sitting on the hideous blue chair with Kelly relaxed into his side, her face pressed into his neck, eyes closed. He was looking down at her and his face was so full of love that Cat's stomach clenched again. Maybe she should try the TENS machine on herself.

Instead she boosted herself up on the bed and used her phone to google 'how to use a TENS machine'. By the time Kelly's next contraction started, she would be good to go.

'Tell me things,' Kelly said a while later. There'd been a few more contractions – Cat wasn't sure how many exactly – and Sean had been sent away to buy an orange Calippo, which Kelly had decided was the only thing she could possibly tolerate.

'What about?'

'Your life. Things that aren't this hospital or a person inside me trying to get out. How's Harvey?'

'He... I haven't... I do have something to tell you actually, but I don't think—'

'Tell me. Now.'

'It's a good thing. For me. I think. But I'm not sure if you—'

'There are medical instruments in here, Cat. I'm sure I can find something sharp and kill you.'

'Jesus. OK. God.' Cat took a deep breath. 'OK. So...'

Kelly made a sound that could only be described as a growl.

'Nick offered me a job. In New York. And I've taken it.'

Kelly looked up at Cat from between her arms. She looked like a wolf. If Cat didn't actually know that Kelly was the sweetest person in the world, she might have been quite scared.

'You're fucking not.'

'Listen, I know it's a big step and—'

'Have you told Harvey?' She'd dropped her head again so the question sounded like it was coming from somewhere near her midriff. It was disconcerting.

'Told him what, I—'

'Told him about New York.'

'Yeah, he... yeah.' Cat couldn't think about it. It was for the best, she knew, but she didn't want to think about it.

'OK. I love you, but you're a fucking idiot and I've had enough of it.'

Cat squeaked with indignation, but Kelly held one finger up and she stopped. Cat waited for her to carry on talking, but instead another contraction hit her and she arched on the bed. She really did look like an animal. It was both awesome and terrifying to watch. Cat wouldn't have been surprised if the baby had come firing out of Kelly's foof by the force of her will. Actually maybe she should station herself down the business end, just in case. Kelly groaned and Cat watched her shoulder blades slide down her back like she'd tried and failed to do at yoga.

'OK,' Kelly said, once it was over, 'I'm going to need you to go find Sean in a minute. But first let me tell you why you're a dickhead.'

'I can get him now if—'

'You think everyone always leaves you, but it's you. You're the one who leaves. And I know you do it to protect yourself, but you still do it. You're the pigeon.'

Cat unzipped her lips. She knew she didn't have the key, but fuck it. 'My dad left,' she said. 'Sam left.'

'Your dad left, yes. Twenty years ago. And how long has he spent trying to have a relationship with you, trying to fix things. But you won't let him. And Sam would have taken you with him if you'd asked. I know he would. You know he would. But you didn't ask.'

'I didn't want to go,' Cat said. 'I wanted him to stay. I wanted him to want to stay. For me.'

'You tried to do it to me too,' Kelly said. 'For the first few years after we met, if we even had a cross word you decided we weren't friends any more. And we wouldn't be. If I hadn't kept pulling you back every time you tried to get away. When you stayed with me that time, you—' All the colour drained out of her face. 'Pass me the hat!'

Cat looked around the room in a panic. 'The hat? What fucking hat?'

'Cardboard… sick… thing…'

Cat just managed to spot a receptacle that did indeed look like a cardboard bowler hat and shoved it under Kelly's face just as a stream of puke launched itself out of her mouth and nose. It splashed the back of Cat's hand, but she didn't even wince. Much.

'Sorry I was sick on you,' Kelly said after. 'Can you go get Sean now. And if you see a midwife ask her to pop her head in, eh?'

'I think you've scared them all away, but I'll do what I can.'

Cat found Sean in the canteen, working on his laptop.

'I can't believe you're working,' she said, sitting next to him. 'She's not... she hasn't—'

'Nah, she just puked and now she wants some of your sweet lovin'.'

'Is she any closer, do you think?'

Cat leaned to the side and looked at Sean's laptop screen. 'What are you doing?'

His cheeks pinked. 'I was just looking at some holidays. Kel mentioned she'd like a babymoon, so I thought—'

'God,' Cat said. 'You are lovely.'

Sean laughed. 'Hardly. I'm out here and she's—'

'She's dealing with it in her own way. It's not a reflection on you.'

'That's what she said.'

'And you know she's always right. And she wants you now so stop being perfect and get back in there and hold her hand.'

'She keeps going for my balls,' Sean said, as he packed his laptop away. And then blushed even harder.

'Seriously?' Cat said, laughing.

'Yeah. I had to keep backing away. She caught me once and it really hurt.'

'I dunno, Sean.' They walked out of the canteen. 'I think you should sacrifice them for the cause. She said she's not having any more kids so it's not like you need them.'

When they got back to the room, a midwife was in with Kelly, who was back on the chair, up on her knees, and moaning.

'Not going to be long now,' the midwife told Sean and Cat as soon as they walked in.

'Really?' Sean said. 'God. Imagine if I'd missed it cos—'

'Oh, it's not going to be minutes,' the midwife said, 'but it should only be a couple of hours.'

'Jesus,' Cat muttered. She crouched down next to Kelly and waited for the contraction to pass before saying, 'What can I do?'

Kelly shook her head. 'Just. Be here.'

Cat dropped a kiss to her sweaty temple. 'I can do that.'

'You,' the midwife directed Sean, 'come here and make your hands into fists then knead them into the small of her back like this.' She placed Sean's hands on his wife's back and showed him how to press and massage her.

'Oh my godddddddddddd,' Kelly said.

Cat fully expected her to tell him to get the fuck away, but she moaned again and this time it sounded like a good moan.

'Yeah?' Sean said.

'Jesus Christ,' Kelly said, twisting her body to look at him over her shoulder. She didn't quite make it. 'Why haven't you been doing that all day?'

'I didn't know—'

'Don't stop!' Kelly said.

Cat found a footstool and dragged it across the room so Sean could sit directly behind Kelly and carry on massaging.

'You're in love with him, you know,' Kelly said a few minutes later. Her eyes were closed and she looked more relaxed than she had for hours.

'Sean? I mean, he's great. And he obviously gives good massage if your sex noises are anything to go by, but—'

'Not Sean. Dickhead. Harvey.'

'Oh my god,' Cat said. 'I don't! I barely know him.' Her stomach twisted again. Where was that vom hat?

'Babe, that's enough,' Kelly told Sean. 'Cat, help me up.'

Cat grasped the top of Kelly's arm and kept her steady while she swung her legs round. 'I'm going to try walking a bit.'

'Where?'

'Just in here. You can help.'

The room wasn't small but it wasn't really big enough for walking. In five steps they were at the door. Kelly pressed both hands against it and bent from the waist, dropping her head again.

'Are you—' Cat didn't even need to finish the question. Kelly was definitely having another contraction.

'What does it feel like?' she asked, once it was over.

'I'll tell you, but don't think you're changing the subject. We're back on you in a minute. It feels like my entire body's in a vice. And just as it becomes so unbearable and I think I'm going to die, it starts to release. But the thing is, now I know how it feels so as soon as it starts, I'm already dreading it. That time I tried to picture a mountain and myself going up up up to the top and then I could slide down the other side, but instead there was just black and pain and my brain going "fucking mountain MOUNTAIN".'

'How are you doing this for a second time?'

'Fucking sing it. Don't let me do this again.' She straightened up and took Cat's arm, the two of them walking back towards the window.

'I'm not in love with him,' Cat said, as they approached the door again.

Kelly snorted. 'I knew you wouldn't be able to resist. You are. I know you. I've seen you in love before and that's how I know. And if you throw it away, you might feel safe, but you're going to be so sorry.'

Cat's eyes filled. 'I don't know what—'

'Look,' Kelly said. 'I'm not trying to upset you. I know this is hard to hear. And I know it almost ruined us last time I tried to tell you some of this shit. Promise me we won't let that happen this time? Cos fuck knows I'm going to need you if I ever get this demon child out of me.'

'You'll need me more if you don't,' Cat mumbled.

Kelly laughed. 'God. Imagine the promo possibilities though. *How to Raise a Child Inside Your Body*. I'd get a book deal and everything.'

'Oh my god,' Cat said two hours later, staring down at the perfect perfect baby in her best friend's arms. The perfect perfect baby she'd just seen her best friend push out of her own actual body. It had been completely gross, but also the most incredible, life-changing, transformative thing Cat had ever seen. And she'd been to *Hamilton*. Twice.

'I can't believe how beautiful she is,' Cat said. 'She looks like a pea.'

Kelly laughed. 'She does not look like a pea.'

'She does. A perfectly round head. And a sweet little face.'

'Like a pea,' Kelly said, laughing. She dipped her head and kissed the baby's forehead. 'She really is beautiful, isn't she?'

'The most beautiful baby I've ever seen. Arnold was a minger.'

Kelly laughed and immediately burst into tears. 'Poor Arnold.'

'Oh, he'll be fine,' Cat said. 'He knows how much you love him. And he'll get used to Little Pea here eventually.'

'We're not calling her Pea,' Kelly said, wetly. 'We're calling her Mabel.'

'Oh,' Cat said, running a finger along the baby's cheek. 'I love that. She looks like a Mabel.'

'She does,' Sean said, coming back in the room with a tray of lattes.

'Oh my god,' Kelly said, reaching for the coffee. 'I love you.'

Sean put the takeout cup down on the side table and leaned over and kissed her on the mouth. 'I love you.'

'Shall I take the baby?' Cat suggested. 'While you two do your filthy business.'

'You can do,' Kelly said, picking Mabel up and handing her over to Cat. 'Hold her head.'

'I know about the head,' Cat said, snuggling Mabel into the crook of her elbow. 'Hi, baby. You look like a pea. But your name is Mabel. And I'm your Aunty Cat. And you're going to love me so much.'

When she looked up, she found Sean had climbed onto the bed with Kelly and they were both looking at her dopily, lattes in hand.

'Oh god, what.'

'You can't go to New York,' Kelly said. 'I need you.'

'You don't need me. I take up too much of your time. You've got your own kids; you don't need to mother me too.'

'I don't mother you, you idiot. You're my best friend. I'd do anything for you. But not if you go to New York. Then you're on your own.'

'That doesn't even make sense,' Cat said. 'You always say I need to push myself and do more and commit to things. Going to New York is all of that!'

'Yeah. But for all the wrong reasons. It's running away. And you need to stop doing that. You know how you say everyone always leaves you? Well, you are not allowed to leave me. I'm not having it.'

Cat dropped her forehead down onto Kelly's shoulder. 'I'm sorry I'm such a mess.'

'But you're my mess.' She kissed her temple. 'And when you've finished your coffee you need to go and see Harvey,' Kelly said.

'Maybe,' Cat said.

But she knew she wouldn't. She was moving to New York. Starting again. Everything was already arranged.

She wasn't going to back out now.

CHAPTER THIRTY-ONE

When Cat got home, all she wanted was a hot shower and to crawl into bed. She smelled like hospital, sick, and baby poo, and she'd almost fallen asleep in the cab back. It had all been worth it though; she couldn't stop looking at the photos of Mabel and Kelly on her phone. Every time she thought about leaving them to go to New York, her eyes filled with tears.

She could hear conversation in the living room and thought about sneaking past so she didn't have to deal with Georgie and Pete, but there really wasn't a way to get to her bedroom without being seen, so she took a deep breath and pushed open the door. But it wasn't Pete Georgie was talking to. It was her dad.

As Cat got closer, he dad stood and reached his arms out as if to hug her, then seemed to change his mind and grabbed her upper arms instead, squeezing lightly.

'Sorry for turning up out of the blue like this.'

Cat was glad he was holding her arms because at least she knew this was really happening. She felt spaced out and bewildered.

'I'm off to work then,' Georgie said, throwing Cat a confused look. 'Nice meeting you, Cat's dad.'

'I thought you'd be back in Australia by now,' Cat said once Georgie had left and they'd both sat down.

'I was meant to be,' he said. 'But I felt like shit about what happened in New York. And also I realised I didn't want to go home again without seeing you, talking to you.'

Cat's throat felt tight. She swallowed. 'I've been avoiding you. That wasn't fair.'

Her dad nodded. 'I get it though. I haven't always been a great dad.' He laughed, dryly. 'That's an understatement.'

'Can I ask you something?' Cat said, her chest feeling like it was about to crack.

'Course.'

'Why did you go?'

Her dad rubbed his face with one large hand. 'What did your mum tell you?'

'Not much. Not that I can remember anyway. I thought she told me the reasons, but I'm not sure if she actually did, if maybe I made it up myself. I remember her getting a letter and I knew it was from you because it had an Australian stamp and I was excited. But when Mum opened it, she went into her bedroom, and I could hear her crying.'

Her dad shook his head. 'Jesus. I'm sorry, Cat. That's not... a child shouldn't...'

'It's OK,' Cat said. Even though it wasn't.

Her dad blew out a long breath and screwed his eyes closed before saying, 'She was supposed to come with me.' He opened his eyes again and looked directly at Cat. 'You both were. I went out there to find somewhere for us to live – I had a job sorted already – and then once I found the place, you and your mum were going to come out and join me.'

Cat stared at him. She couldn't believe it was true. 'So why didn't we?'

'Your mum changed her mind. Said she didn't love me any more. Said she didn't realise until I left. She thought it maybe would be different in Australia. But once I'd gone, she realised she wasn't happy and she wanted to stay in the UK.'

Cat couldn't catch her breath. 'Why didn't you come back?' she asked eventually.

Her dad shook his head. 'I was heartbroken. I couldn't even think. Also I didn't have the money for a ticket. My original plan was to work enough to save the money. But the longer I worked, the more it seemed more sensible to stay.' He shook his head. 'Not more sensible, not really. Easier. Easier than coming home and seeing your mum and seeing you and being faced with everything I'd lost.'

'I'm sorry,' Cat said. It was all she could think of.

'Me too.'

Cat spent the entire day in bed. She cried until she fell asleep, then woke up and cried until she fell asleep again. She couldn't believe she'd spent pretty much her entire life believing her dad had left when he hadn't at all. She didn't blame her mum – she knew she'd been trying to protect her, do what was best for both of them, all of them perhaps – but how had Cat spent so long reinforcing and preserving a story she'd told herself that wasn't even true? And if she was wrong about that, what else might she be wrong about?

In the evening when Georgie and Pete came home and started painting again, listening to obnoxiously loud music, Cat dragged herself to the shower and stood under the water for a long time. She'd fucked up. But she was going to fix it.

'I think I'm in love with Harvey,' Cat told Sam after work a few days later.

She'd finally friended him on Facebook and they'd messaged a little before she'd asked him to meet her at the pub near her office.

'Jesus Christ,' Sam said. 'You didn't want to give me a bit of warning?'

Cat winced. 'Sorry. I'm trying this new thing where I say what I mean and tell people how I feel and I haven't really mastered it yet. You're not... it doesn't bother...'

Sam pulled a face. 'I mean, it's not what I'd choose.'

'I know. I'm sorry. It wasn't planned, if that helps at all?'

Sam laughed, ducking his head. 'You know what? It doesn't really.'

'No. I didn't really think it would.'

'But I did wonder. He mentions you a lot.'

Something warmed in Cat's chest at the thought that Harvey may possibly, impossibly, feel the same way.

'Does he know?' Sam asked.

Cat shook her head.

'Mum's going to be pleased. She misses you.'

Cat laughed. 'God. Don't get ahead of yourself. He might not want me back.'

Sam's mouth twisted and he shook his head again. 'He will. Why wouldn't he?'

'Well, that's kind of where you come in. When's your next show?'

CHAPTER THIRTY-TWO

'He's not here,' she told Kelly. 'He didn't come.'

'He's probably just late. Don't worry about it.' Kelly, on her first night out post-baby, was sitting in the corner of the dressing room with a glass of wine, smiling at Cat serenely.

Cat shook her head. 'Maybe Sam told him I was going to be here and he decided not to come.'

'Sam would have told you if he'd done that.'

'He'd be here by now if he was coming. He's very punctual.'

'You're wigging out,' Kelly said, putting her hands on Cat's shoulders. 'Take a deep breath. He'll be here.'

Cat's eyes pricked with tears. 'He has to be here. I want to tell him—'

'I know you do,' Kelly said, squeezing the tops of Cat's arms. 'But even if he doesn't come tonight—'

Cat squeaked.

'He will!' Kelly said. 'But even if he doesn't, you can still tell him. You have to tell him.'

Cat nodded. She felt like she was going to be sick or wet herself. Her palms were sweating and her legs were actually trembling. She couldn't believe she was putting herself through this again.

'You're going to be great,' Kelly told her, dipping her head to force Cat to look into her eyes. 'You're going to be charming and hilarious and hot.'

Cat snorted.

'And Harvey will be there and you'll tell him how you feel and everything will be OK. Trust me. I've pushed two people out of my fanny; I'm very wise.'

'Those things are unconnected,' Cat said. 'But you are anyway.' She rooted through her bag looking for her jeans. 'I'm scared.'

'That means you're doing it right,' Kelly said.

Cat's phone buzzed with a message. Her dad, wishing her luck. He was back in Australia, but they'd set a weekly date to chat, either on WhatsApp or the phone. It had been nice, getting to know each other properly.

'Where do you even get this crap from anyway? Some inspirational Instagram account?'

'Feel the fear and do it anyway,' Kelly said. 'It's a whole thing. Also: outside your comfort zone is where the magic happens. That one is actually from Instagram. But that doesn't mean it's not true.'

'Was it attributed to Marilyn Monroe?' Cat said, yanking her jeans out of the bag and immediately pulling her leggings down. 'Or Abraham Lincoln.'

'Why are you getting changed?'

'Cos my leggings keep rolling down.'

'You said you didn't want to wear those jeans cos they go up your arse.'

'They do.' Cat stepped into them and wiggled them up her legs. The knees of the jeans were ripped open. 'But that's better than rolled-down leggings.'

'Haven't you got any clothes that, you know, fit you?'

'You know I haven't.' Her phone buzzed again. Nick this time. He'd been disappointed when Cat had turned down the job, but he understood. And he was back in London the following week. They were going to have lunch.

'I truly don't know how you live,' Kelly said.

'I might not for much longer. I might die out there.'

'People are going to laugh. People always laugh.'

'I don't mean comedy die. I mean actual die. I might just walk out there and keel over.'

'You won't. You'll walk out there. You'll do your set. You'll talk to Harvey and then you two will ride off into the sunset on a white horse.'

'The sun set, like, four hours ago. And did you bring a horse cos I didn't?'

'OK then, an Uber. Back to his flat.'

Cat took a shaky breath. 'What if he doesn't want me?'

'He will. He does. Trust me.'

There was a knock at the door and Cat called, 'Come in,' without looking up from where she'd started rummaging in her bag for the chunk of rose quartz she'd bought after her first ever stand-up and thought of as a good luck charm.

'Hey,' a male voice said.

Cat smiled and turned towards the door. But it wasn't Harvey. It was Sam.

'You've got five minutes,' he told Cat.

'Fuck,' Cat said. 'God.'

'You'll be fine,' Sam said. 'Actually, you'll be great. You always were.'

'Thanks,' Cat said, trying to take a deep breath, but it kept getting stuck behind her breastbone. 'See you after?'

'I think you'll probably be busy after,' Kelly said.

'God,' Cat said. 'Shut up.'

'I did stand-up before,' Cat said, looking at the first row of the crowd. She saw a young-looking woman smiling back at her brightly, encouraging, and a man with folded arms and that 'impress me' expression on his face. She remembered that from last time.

'But then I stopped.'

She still couldn't see Harvey. Maybe he really hadn't come.

'I thought I stopped because I wasn't enjoying it any more. But I actually stopped because my boyfriend was also a stand-up and I was better than him.'

A ripple of laughter.

'No, I'm serious. He was good, but I was better than him. And we'd do shows and I'd get bigger laughs and I'd apologise. And once I tried to give him some tips. He didn't like that. I always thought men would appreciate it if you tried to, you know, improve them. But they don't. Did you know that? I guess it might've worked if I was five gay guys. But I'm not. I'm just one straight woman. So he didn't. Didn't learn to make guacamole or do a French tuck or reunite with his estranged father or anything. He just withheld sex a bit.'

The laughs were getting bigger now and Cat could feel herself uncurling, her shoulders straightening. She'd always felt sort of powerful onstage. She'd almost forgotten. She glanced over to the right and saw Gemma Jewell leaning against the wall. Gemma fucking Jewell was watching her perform. She knew she was probably here for Sam, but even so.

'Actually that bit about his estranged father isn't true,' she said, tearing her eyes away from her all-time favourite comedian. Who was there. Watching her. 'He has a lovely father. And mother. And brother. It was hard for me to finish with him because of his family. If I could've kept them, I would've. You know when you split up with someone and you have to decide who keeps which friends? Like – "I want Donna and Jack cos they're great on a night out but you can have Suzy and Paul cos they insist on showing us their holiday photos and there's always one of one or both of them naked and they say 'Whoops! Don't know how that slipped in there!'" Well, I would have liked to have kept his family. But that seemed a bit unreasonable. Even for me. But obviously I did have to finish with him. Because I was better at stand-up than he was.

'I should probably stop saying that because he's here. Sorry, Sam. And now I've said his name, just in case there was any doubt.'

'It's all true though,' Sam shouted and Cat barked out a laugh. 'God. Anyway, his family was so great that I did a terrible thing. I fell in love with his brother.'

There was a gasp of shock from the audience and Cat said, 'I know. I'm a terrible person. I was hoping he was going to be here tonight. Not just because it would add drama, but because I haven't actually told him that yet, but I don't think he...'

Shielding her eyes with her hand, she scanned the audience, taking in the various faces looking back at her. She couldn't see him. He really hadn't come. Her chest ached with it. And now she had to somehow get to the end of this set without crying.

She swallowed down the lump in her throat. Took a deep breath.

And then he was there. Standing towards the back of the room. Looking right at her. And he was smiling.

CHAPTER THIRTY-THREE

'You need to get up,' Cat said, crawling up the bed and bracketing Harvey's hips with her thighs.

'I would,' he said, smiling up at her. 'But you're sitting on me.'

She rolled her eyes. 'I am *now*. I wasn't before. You've had plenty of time to get up and get a shower—'

'Mm,' Harvey said, shifting down the bed and pulling Cat down on top of him. 'A shower sounds good.'

'Alone. I haven't got time for a shower. I've got a house-warming party to prepare for.'

'Oh, come on. It's all done. And even if it's not, no one will care.' He rolled her so he was on top and kissed the side of her neck. She wriggled out from underneath him and stood up. 'I need to go and buy ice.'

He stretched out on the bed, the duvet down around his waist, and looked up at her. 'Ice? Interesting.'

'Oh god,' Cat said. And got back into bed.

'Are you licking my dimple?' Harvey asked a little later, when Cat had decided no one was going to be bothered about ice, it'd be fine.

'I can't believe this,' Cat said, not for the first time, resting her chin on Harvey's chest and pressing her fingers in turn into his dimple to see which one would fit.

'My dimple?' Harvey asked. His eyes were closed, but his lips were curved into a smile.

She gave up examining his dimple and dipped her head to kiss his shoulder instead, before letting her lips drift down his arm to his elbow. 'Do you know you've got sexy elbows? I didn't know that was a thing.'

'I don't think it is. Seems a bit niche.'

She wanted to fit her mouth round it and maybe suck a bit, but that seemed weird, even for her.

'Harvey,' she said, propping herself up above him and looking into his eyes. 'I've told you that I'm in love with you, right?'

Harvey smiled slowly, sliding his hands down her back. 'Once or twice, yeah. But feel free to tell me again.'

Harvey was right: everything was ready by the time people started to arrive. Kelly and Sean were first. Sean had the baby strapped to his front in a carrier.

'Look at you!' Cat said, dropping a kiss to Mabel's forehead and then another to Sean's cheek.

'Sorry we're late,' Kelly said. 'We had to go home because someone pooed.'

'Sean!' Cat said.

'It wasn't me!' Arnold yelled from behind his dad's legs.

'Aha!' Cat said, bending to kiss the top of his head. 'I didn't see you there. Ooh, you smell like...' She took a big sniff. 'Ketchup and strawberries and... McDonald's. Have you been to McDonald's?!'

'That was the other stop,' Kelly said. 'Sorry, but he was hangry and I didn't want to bring him in here kicking off.'

'The thing is,' Cat told Arnold, 'I hope you're still a bit hungry cos I made jelly.'

'I LOVE JELLY,' Arnold yelled.

'You can eat it all then,' Cat said.

'Yeah, there's no way that's going to end well,' Kelly said. 'Come on then. Give us the tour.'

Cat held out her arms. 'This is pretty much it.'

The flat was one main room with a kitchenette at the end.

'I'd show you the bedroom, but Harvey's getting changed and... actually that's worth seeing, follow me.'

'I'm done,' Harvey said, appearing through the door and crossing the small room to shake hands with Sean, kiss Kelly, do the complicated handshake he and Arnold had worked out together, and say a very sweet 'Hi, baby,' to Mabel.

Cat was surprised at how easily Harvey had fitted into her friendship with Kelly and Sean. He and Sean got on brilliantly – they'd been out together socially without Kelly and Cat and Kelly was delighted that Sean had a male friend she didn't hate. Cat had thought it would make her feel trapped, but it didn't. It made her feel safe.

The door opened again and Harvey's parents came in and immediately started fussing over Arnold and the baby.

'Sam said to say hi,' Harvey's mum told Cat.

Cat still felt a prickle of awkwardness whenever Harvey's mum mentioned Cat's previous relationship with her other son, but it was getting easier all the time.

'You've spoken to him?'

'Skyped. This morning. Well, night-time there.'

Sam was in Australia for the comedy festival.

'Is he having a good time?'

'Loving it,' Jan said. 'Now can I have a cuddle with that baby, do you think?'

As Sean wrestled Mabel out of the carrier to hand her to Jan, there was another knock on the door and Cat opened it to find her dad standing there. She'd seen him a few times over the past couple of months, but always on neutral ground. It still wasn't easy, but it was getting easier. Particularly since he insisted he was staying in London now. He'd brought wine and flowers and by the time Cat had opened the wine and put the flowers in water, everyone else had moved out onto the reason she and Harvey had fallen in love with this tiny flat.

They weren't in Central London any more. But they had a terrace. It was almost the same size as the living room and big enough for a small table and a few beanbag chairs with planters around the edge. Cat had hung fairy lights around the railings and she couldn't love it more.

'This is wonderful,' Jan said, holding up her glass. 'To Cat and Harvey's new home.'

Everyone clinked their glasses and Cat leaned into Harvey's side.

'It's so perfect,' Kelly said.

'It really is,' Cat agreed. 'We have coffee out here in the mornings and wine in the evenings...' And they'd almost had sex out there more than once but it was over-looked by at least ten neighbouring flats and neither of their parents needed to know about that.

'And Cat comes out here to fake-smoke,' Harvey said, bumping her with his hip.

'You smoke?' Cat's dad asked, his forehead furrowed with concern.

'Nah,' Cat said. 'Harvey thinks he's funny.'

Harvey pressed a kiss against her temple and she considered asking everyone to leave so they could try to do it on the terrace. Maybe if they arranged a blanket like a tent?

Everyone jumped when Arnold screamed, flailing across the terrace to slam into Kelly's legs.

'What's up?' she said, leaning down to comfort him.

'A bee!' he yelled, his eyes wide with fear.

'Bees are good,' Kelly said. 'You don't need to be scared of bees.'

'As long as you steer clear of their exploding balls,' Cat said. 'Do you think I could do stand-up about exploding bee balls?'

'If anyone could, you could,' Harvey said, wrapping his arms around her waist from behind and resting his chin on her shoulder.

She squeezed him back and looked at Kelly, Sean and Arnold. At Jan cooing over Mabel while Harvey's dad, William, chatted with her dad.

'You OK?' Harvey said, his mouth next to her ear.

'Perfect,' Cat said.

EPILOGUE

'I got you a latte,' Harvey said, when Cat came out of the loo.

She'd been nervous-peeing all morning. She had an interview with a marketing company looking for a Head of Story. She wasn't entirely qualified, but the female manager she'd spoken to on the phone had seemed excited at the idea of having a stand-up comedian working for them, particularly one who was going to be opening for Gemma Jewell's next London show.

Cat leaned against him and he dropped his arm around her shoulder, squeezing her and kissing her temple.

'I don't think I can drink it,' Cat said. 'Too nervous.'

'You'll be brilliant,' Harvey said. 'You always are.'

Cat kissed him, marvelling as she so often did at how much she liked kissing him. How much she liked him full stop.

'And you'll wait for me?' Cat asked.

'I'll be here,' Harvey said. 'I'm not going anywhere.'

And Cat believed him.

A LETTER FROM KERIS

I want to say a huge thank you for choosing to read *The One Who's Not the One*. If you enjoyed it, and want to keep up-to-date with all my latest releases, just sign up at the following link. Your email address will never be shared and you can unsubscribe at any time.

www.bookouture.com/keris-stainton

The One Who's Not the One was so much fun to write and I hope you had fun reading it. If you did I would be very grateful if you could write a review. I'd love to hear what you think, and it makes such a difference helping new readers to discover one of my books for the first time.

I love hearing from my readers – you can get in touch on my Facebook page, through Twitter, Goodreads or my website.

Thanks,
Keris

 www.keris-stainton.com

 keriswritesbooks

 @Keris

ACKNOWLEDGEMENTS

Thank you as always to Abi Fenton and Hannah Sheppard for their encouragement and patience.

Enormous thanks to Emily Holmden Kingsman for the tour.

Hugs to Harry and Joe for being the best.

I wrote this book during a difficult year that also contained so many pockets of fun and joy. Endless thanks and love to my friends for the laughing and crying, singing and dancing, eating and drinking, and so so many high-traffic group chats. Let's do it all again this year (maybe with a bit less crying)

Printed in Great Britain
by Amazon